CHAPEL STREET

CHAPEL STREET

Sam North

GROVE WEIDENFELD

New York

Published by Grove Weidenfeld
A division of Grove Press, Inc.
841 Broadway
New York, New York 10003-4793

Published in Canada by General Publishing Company, Ltd.

First published in Great Britain in 1991 by Martin Secker & Warburg Ltd.

Library of Congress Cataloging-in-Publication Data
North, Sam.
Chapel Street / Sam North.—1st American ed.
p.   cm.
ISBN 0-8021-1466-0
I. Title.
PR6064.0765C4   1992
823'.914—dc20   91-29523
CIP

Manufactured in the United States of America

Printed on acid-free paper

Designed by Irving Perkins Associates

First American Edition 1992

1   3   5   7   9   10   8   6   4   2

CHAPEL
STREET

ONE

ᘛᕽᘚ

T HE HOUSE FOOLED everyone.

It stood, solid on a solid street, part of a row of creamy Georgian residences in one of the wealthiest business districts. From the outside it appeared even more magnificently rich than its neighbors. Two classical columns proclaimed the outstanding importance of the building, and upheld a useful porch over the steps up to the front door. However, for a reason that wasn't at all sinister, the façade was bluffing.

The people who walked the street in front of the house were mostly wealth-creating pedestrians, chasing business or collecting their cars from the garage in the mews opposite. They wore suits and carpet-creeping shoes; they carried briefcases, newspapers, umbrellas for the rain. It was a strange conformity that the years of development had wrought, this suit with its pockets, the shirt with a little collar, these heels and stockings and skirts: a front with which to breast the world, an investment. It was impossible to think that each person was different, when they all looked so much the same.

Santay, barreling along Chapel Street, the wind behind him, thought, "They all look strung up by their ties."

Every now and again someone like Santay would come along and break the mold. It was not difficult: a pair of jeans, an orange anorak or a book in your hand, any of these would do it. The uniformed traffickers of the street would class such unlikely apparitions as interlopers, tourists, or people lost, or students, but then they'd be treated to a mild surprise. The outsiders turned into that house, the one with the porch, the outstanding architectural example, the only one with the pillars.

Santay's behavior as he stopped outside the house provoked more than a lifted eyebrow or frown. It caused concern. He knew this, but he was by now used to indulging in small-scale perversity. It was his privilege. He took the same license as old people and lunatics. Pedestrians crossed the road rather than have to negotiate him throwing the cricket ball at the front door. Sometimes he would fail to trap the ball as it dribbled back off the bounce, but he fielded it all right, mostly. He had been good at sport.

TWO

It WAS WET, that autumn. As always there were thousands seeking shelter.

Safe from the rain beneath the civilized portal, prospective tenants would knock and wait, astounded at the thought of living in such luxury. They might have glimpsed the fixtures and fittings available in the other houses, through the windows or as people peeled off their streaming macs in open doorways, revealing that curious human architecture: twin columns holding a fluted waist, surmounted by plinth-like shoulders, topped by a more or less decorative head. When Molly answered their knock, however, opening the mansion-quality front door, they would find no smooth acreage of carpet, no chandelier, no Regency hall table with a silver platter on it for the letters. Instead, immediately out of the gloom, before they even set one foot over this particular threshold, there came at them the smell of old vegetables and soup. When their eyes had dilated to meet the lack of daylight (and what light there was seemed as old as the wallpaper, as though it had been hanging about in the corners, caught and held by the cobwebs and failing slowly with age), they could see that this place was a riot, an imbroglio of *stuff*.

All people carry some baggage with them, but whoever lived here hadn't let go of anything. The hall was a store for old boxes and bags of varying size and age, precariously stashed on each side up to the height of a man's shoulder, with a tunnel down the middle which just exceeded the width of the landlady's hips. She could scrape by with an inch or two to spare, there being only so much clearance because she swayed from side to side.

If they decided to continue (the more dithery prospectors turned away there and then), they'd be asked to follow Molly's shabby corduroy trousers, passing first the closed door to her room on their right, and then a second doorway, also on the right-hand side. At this point, when the house had them firmly in its interior, when it had closed behind them, impressed its atmosphere onto them heavily like a homemade blanket, they would take to the perilous stairs and descend to the basement kitchen for an extended interview with the landlady.

Molly was waiting outside the kitchen door, ready to introduce an unknown youth. She overheard Mrs. Gorse talking loudly. "We *must* believe," the latter was saying, as urgently as if it were a wartime escape plan, "we have to believe. Or we die. *But not in a silly way.* D'you understand? I can't have fanatics in this house. I'm sorry."

Two people came out dressed in orange cotton, followed by Gabriella, who was blushing.

Molly's turn. She stepped inside.

"Skim," she said.

"Who?"

"Skim."

"Yes yes. Skim. Of course!" Mrs. Gorse waved at Molly, who retreated, under orders, leaving them to it.

Skim felt actively hemmed in. A family-size table stood askew in the middle of the room covered in papers and kitchen utensils; a dresser backed up against the far wall, crowded with crockery, supporting a monster German television set; piles of books teetered everywhere; a coat-stand offered several limp victims hung by the neck; picture postcards, bills, letters—all manner of paper bits—were pinned to the wall; a sink waited for work between a double drainer; the stove was blowing hotly in the recess; there was a sofa covered by a rug; the landlady herself sat round as a plum (she always wore black), grinning like a Moroccan salesman. The kitchen had a poised excitement to it, as though seconds before everything had been flying about in a magical turbulence and as soon as you turned away it would happen again; you'd glance back to find yourself somewhere different—in a chalet on the south coast?

Mrs. Gorse welcomed Skim. All her moods were running in the same direction that day. A stampede of good humors! She took in his height, his bigness, the wagging knee. Skim had arrived. She unsheathed her teeth and hid her eyes almost completely when she used her smile, as she did now, listening to him give his name and explain his job. Breathing heavily and using furniture to launch herself from one spot to another, she fetched him his keys. She bulged with a bigger grin inside than she had out front, feeling the cool fringe of metal passing into his hands.

"And remember," she said, "while you're in this house you have to be careful, you men, to control that missile in your trousers."

"Right," said Skim loudly, shy of the sudden vulgarity, but Mrs. Gorse was already ahead.

"You know, of course," she gasped, "that the world will end because of stupidity? Not braveness, or accident, not even ignorance, but stupidity? A stupid ending! This I can't stand. With all this knowledge, with *facts* as common as potatoes!" She lifted her hands in the air. "Satellite TV. Rockets all over space, in other galaxies now, even. Like

7

fireworks in the air all the time, celebrating so much *stupid* science. A maelstrom!" She dropped her arms to lean on the table. Despite all this she was still cheerful.

Then her face dropped. "Molly!" she barked, in the direction of the door, "Molly! Gabriella?"

They waited until Molly appeared, dragging her corduroys with her, a matching pair of willowy animals.

"In with Marek," Mrs. Gorse ordered, "to share with Marek. Rent in advance, one week, Saturdays."

Skim was taken to his room.

Mrs. Gorse imagined the tools of his trade growing into a litter on the table: there would be latex, lengths of wire, the scalpel knives and glue guns, the clay and the hardboard. She could see all this.

Gabriella had accused her. "You are a witch!" she'd said. A witch? If she was a witch, where was her book of spells? She would be taking Skim and his tools and the keys and the train timetable, she would be throwing them all into the cauldron, into a frog stew, and stirring it all up, wouldn't she? Then she'd have to get in herself, up to her ears, swim around, climb back out in a dress of printed flowers, with a hat on her head . . . She laughed out loud, catching the look of disapproval from Hawkins who was running his side along the radiator.

She returned to what she had been doing before she'd been interrupted—the vegetables lolled on the table waiting for her knife. She watched her hands sever a carrot. "I'm sorry," she bullied it, "I can't help you, I don't know, I don't know enough, not even now . . ." She felt renewed sadness.

"Age," she murmured. The scene blurred in front of her. She began to travel away.

Going very gently, Mrs. Gorse approached the moment of her death. Slowly, hidden behind closed eyelids, she crept up, inch by inch, crawling past the moment when her body would start to relax toward deadweight, beyond the last sleepy billowing of her lungs, until she arrived at the very instant her heart would stop, and the blood settle in her veins.

She felt Time's gravity slipping.

There it was, her very own death . . .

The sudden thrill made her retreat; she backtracked furiously as though pursued.

She gave commands: "Reverse! Back! . . ."

With relief she felt herself gaining weight. The familiar authority of her body, encased in black, worked as an anchor; it dragged her back to the here and now. She heard the calling of her cat, Hawkins.

She found herself still standing with her feet splayed. The knife was in her hand, the blade pushing through the wrinkled carrots. She was trembling, but with such a fine oscillation as to make it more like a vibration.

Safe in the middle of her basement kitchen, she promised herself (as always) never to do that again.

She remembered when it had started, Time's trick on her: April 15, 1938, Berlin. Small and frightened, she'd been staring through the darkness to where the railway track first described itself in the light blooming from the tunnel openings, which were out of sight at either end of the curve.

There was the certainty of the voices, but the question of which direction the sound came from. The injured man behind her was silent. She'd waited, poised on the tracks, striving to hear. She was waiting so nervously, waiting so hard, that Time slowed up, didn't pass by as usual, pressed in on her harder and harder, locking her off onto the nub of a distended moment . . . It was then that Time (ambitious to be *involved*) had managed to poke a finger through and tickle a precarious way in. She'd felt it, that lack of gravity, the going-away of all horizons . . .

9

And now, that a woman of her unique talents would be getting no special treatment at the moment of death! It would be for her, as it was for everyone else, a leap into unknowledge.

It was always disheartening to be reminded that she would die in a room with brown walls. Brown? Her least favorite, the color of mud, dead leaves, boredom.

There was something else that made her angry: she knew she was grander, more important than any actress standing on a world stage, but she had no audience, nor would she ever have one.

Meanwhile she was to go about doing the normal things. The vegetables. The long letter to her comrade in Berlin. The washing. The business of the visitors staying in her rooms.

With a rough scrape she cleared the board and shifted the next carrot under the knife. Each movement of her hands triggered multiple layers of *déjà vu*. She prepared the bargain vegetables with the old, old knowledge that she had been here before, several times, and this wasn't a case of one side of her brain tripping up the other. She only knew where she was in her life by recognizing the sudden weight of her body. She had exhausted every moment up and down the length of her life's span.

Her eyes, black and hard and dry as stones, blinked angrily at the frustration of having such a pointless, unique, brilliant . . . what? What was it? Gift? Trick? Sometimes it had seemed like a curse. But now that Skim had arrived . . .

Hawkins walked across the table, eyeing her, moving smoothly as though propelled by the draft on his lifted tail.

"Retirement, Hawkins!" said Mrs. Gorse, chucking the cat under its chin. "What d'you think of that? Just a fat old lady like any other, with a big-screen TV, and troubles with my blood, and my bowels, and my brain. It will be like being retired, for me."

A GRANDMOTHER CLOCK stood up on the first-floor landing. The sonorous tocking of this ancient contraption, reliable, steadily measuring the mood of the place, belied Time's true character here.

Five-thirty p.m. Oh yes, *Time* was in the house. Time wasn't just waiting, wasn't just hanging around.

THREE

DIFFERENT CHARACTERS WOULD appear to answer the *crack!* made by Santay's cricket ball against the front door. If they didn't know him they responded in the prescribed manner; he knew it backward and upside-down. Most people first of all experienced some sort of jolt in the back of the head. It must be like that; he imagined it as being an electric charge. Almost simultaneously came the urgent effort to dampen it, to make it invisible to him. There had been for a fraction of a second a wildness in their system; they would haul back to control it, but it would be given away by a sudden hitching of some muscle in the face (usually somewhere round the jaw, which he could easily see from his position below), and an unnatural sprint into over-friendliness. The battle and confusion could go on for an indefinite time. He preferred that, however, to people like Molly who tried to join his side, who almost wanted to get in the bloody chair and ride along with him.

"You don't have to use the cricket ball," she said to him. "If you tell me when you're coming back I can make sure I look out for you. Or I'm sure we can extend the doorbell down to street level for you."

12

She claimed to have more than one pair of corduroys, but Santay was suspicious.

He'd never got off to a good start with Molly. He had tried several times; over and over again came this effort at a new beginning, but it never worked. It was his fault as much as hers. Part of the problem of his constantly needing help was putting up with it when he got it. He and Molly had immediately found themselves engaged in a polite war, the battleground one of extraordinary intimacy. He didn't want help, he resented even the minimum necessary. Molly on the other hand wanted him to need as much help as she wanted to give, but there was an ugliness to her charity. She saved it like money, favor after favor adding up to go toward some starchy target of self-worth that she'd set herself. This prickly push-and-pull between them made her generosity charmless, never fun or funny. Her increasing store of righteousness was sinister, and hidden, and her motives were sad, because she was ugly. There was no competition between them on that score. Santay would rather have had no arms than have to walk around with her face.

Santay considered her new offer of help. "But I'm in training," he replied, "I might be asked to join the England team."

He had a quasi-cantankerous style that he used for dealing with her. She understood this. She understood everything. She gave him a fond smile and withdrew.

The other tenants, if they stayed for a month or more, became accustomed to helping Santay. The occasions added up to become a ritual of perfect homeliness, like switching their kettle on or closing a door behind them. It was toward such a state of affairs that he was always aiming with the people around him. He saw it as breaking people in, training them to be ordinary with him. Some people never got there; they stayed wild.

He liked the challenge of new people, but early autumn

13

was the silly season—there were so many seeking lodgings at that time of year.

Skim, for instance, blundered into Santay's room by mistake and remained, halted, looking down at him like he was a wounded animal or a smashed-up car.

Santay had his commonplace "specimen" feeling. Grueling. While he waited for Skim to come round from the reaction (and it felt like a wait, like a long time, although it was probably only a couple of beats) he became angry. He asked, "What's up?" in a falsely neutral tone, and with immediate regret. Now that he had lost control even to such a marginal extent things could only get nastier for him. The discomfort threatened to turn acute; humor seemed an impossible resource.

Skim replied, "I thought this was the toilet . . ." and then paused to consider something, how to avoid Santay, how to explain himself, maybe.

"I hate seeing bad luck," he continued, abruptly.

"I hate being it," Santay replied.

The door closed. Santay heard the man's feet dropping heavily on the stairs down to the basement. He listened to the muffled (and doomed) attempt to close the toilet door down there. Solitude settled gradually, mercifully, but mixed with a familiar twinge of regret at being left alone.

A new face. The force of the reaction had run across his expression; you could see the passage of its energy leave a mark like an animal's run through a cornfield. Thinking about it, as he sat there waiting for *anything* to happen, Santay eventually approved. It had been a big face, set on a body that had filled the doorframe, but the expression had been free to do what it wanted; that was refreshing. So many people's faces were hedged about with rules, boxed in until no expression was allowed.

He wheeled himself over to the computer and fired it up.

14

The machine bleeped a welcome and ran up an opening command: *Please set time and date.* He always ignored this command on principle. What did the date matter to him? Time passed over his head; he could do nothing with it, and it didn't seem to want to do anything with him.

FOUR

THE LANDLADY WAS shouting. Santay heard the wind of it blow round the house. Her voice had such reach, it agitated the air all the way up through the staircase. It could blast through the mansion-quality walls, it had that much of an edge to it. Everyone stopped to listen. The long-stay tenants in the lofty rooms above, the worried night-by-night travelers packed into the basement, all were arrested in the middle of their various actions: carrying a soiled mug to the sink, making a bed, writing home.

Molly was scratching an outbreak of itch.

Santay had no need to stop doing anything because he was doing nothing, massaging his wrecked knees at the most. He couldn't make out the rattling rows of words, but guessing had become a required skill for someone of his curiosity. The different tones of the landlady's voice corresponded to a code. The jet-fighter screams were accusations; the antique machine-gun sound was a rhetorical question; then the rumbling came, for the final complaints. Something to do with . . . Gabriella's boyfriend coming to stay soon, and the house not being clean enough for her to deserve such a dirty privilege.

Gabriella had made the mistake of entering into an agreement with the landlady, offering to clean the house instead of paying rent. She'd also made another, much graver error: she'd grown up to be a young woman. Mrs. Gorse perceived Gabriella's healthiness as an unbelievable arrogance.

"Respect!" cried Mrs. Gorse, glaring at the girl, astounded at the profusion of dark hair sprouting from the plastic clip on her head. "If I have respect for you, I must have respect back. You cannot use this place as a love parlor. I am not Madame Pompadour!"

The row was winding down. Gabriella knew better than to say anything. She kept her virginity to herself. Whatever she said might be an excuse for her employer to veer off in a new direction.

"So please," said Mrs. Gorse, "zip it up." She nodded at Gabriella to indicate that the interview was over.

After a while the house started to move again.

It was understood that Gabriella took a break when she was meant to be cleaning Santay's room. He tidied up after himself (laboriously) and offered her a cup of tea to get some words and her energetic but sad eyes looking at him.

"Oh my God!" she exclaimed, sitting down on his bed with a thump. (The bed was too strong not to hit back.) Her heavy, well-separated eyebrows rose comically up and outward.

"She is a witch," continued Gabriella, rolling her eyes. "I tell her she is a witch, to her face, but she never take any notice of my ... of my explosions. She just 'as 'er own explosion, and then carry on as though she's no to do with the problem!"

"What is the problem?" asked Santay, recognizing his cue.

"Ohh ... is Marek ... Mar-ek ... !" she moaned, delighted. She clasped the unfortunately empty air.

"Marek?"

"New boy," she replied, "in that one, you know ..." She

17

dabbed her finger impatiently through the air in the direction of their room. "Sharing with the other one, Skim."

"I haven't met Marek," said Santay, uncomfortable in his chair, not looking forward to hearing the praise of another man sung so loudly in his room, in front of him, with his knees.

"He is so . . ." she said, greedily, "so . . . ohh!" and then she threw herself backward onto his bed and, continuing the roll, lifted her legs as high as her jeans would allow before letting them drop sideways. Santay blinked twice but didn't manage to stop himself from catching sight of the junction of frayed seams that met in a neat cross between her legs. What would it be like there, hidden in that tuck of flesh? Was it fabulous, or difficult? What sort of temperature would it be? Where all those seams met . . . He could imagine, but that was like looking without her permission. It was ghoulish that he should want to investigate, he thought. Did he really want to? He thought again about his curiosity habit. His fear was of being left out, and therefore he was impossibly *interested,* so thirstily inquisitive it had for him the quality of an emotion. He silently accused himself—"Pervert!"—for indulging in the sight of her seams. He felt ugly, ungracious.

Gabriella sat upright and continued to explain the new dilemma of having a boyfriend about to arrive from far away when she was in love with someone else. The boyfriend would knock on the door. What could she say to him? Should she tell him about Marek?

Santay simulated a Marek for himself. His idea was formed by the plain Eastern Bloc allure of the name, and by the fact that on mentioning it Gabriella had flung herself on her back and stuck her legs in the air, looking like a turkey that Santay had seen in a similar position dramatically jammed in the oven one Christmas Day. Marek would have to be a brooding working-class hero with a wide face.

Later, when Gabriella had gone and he was bundled up

18

in his own reserve, Santay wondered if he shouldn't perhaps stop himself from being so nosy; perhaps then he wouldn't be feeling empty and insubstantial as the armful of air Gabriella had earlier clasped to herself.

But no, it wasn't that. It was just that with each new friend that Gabriella added to her list, he suffered loss, he owned proportionately less of her.

He often welcomed isolation, but if it went too far it could hurt so harshly that he wanted to rape somebody's mind, almost anybody's, just to get out of his own; and if he hung his isolation about himself and moved among other people with it visible, it was like being in the middle of a barren continent that moved with him, keeping him at its center, while all other people were beyond its distant frontiers (except for people like Molly, who seemed to get let in somehow and aimed straight for him just to make it worse).

Increasingly he felt like he was sitting on his own life (not hatching it, but stifling it), mothering the moments along in the hope of something happening to him.

To him! What hope was there?

FIVE

Mrs. Gorse carried the basket of washing out to the backyard and dropped it beneath the line. She placed her fists on her hips and heaved back onto her haunches. Her angry face aimed briefly at the sky.

"It won't rain," she thought.

Yet as she cast the first article of clothing the rear end of her brain jumped and turned in frustration. Her mouth gripped the two pegs, didn't want to let them go. A hiss came from between her teeth but it was futile. The washingline danced in front of her, flagged with garments. She just had to get on with it.

Santay, meanwhile, was going out: Victoria Station. It was an obstacle course. Some of the curbs were steep, but he had practiced often enough. He stared at the faces that passed above him to judge how they would be judging him. From some of these intently busy figures he would be demanding help if it was necessary. Once he'd rounded the end of Chapel Street he screwed round in his seat to check that Molly wasn't following him.

20

The top half of his body grew hot; his hands sweated in the fingerless gloves. He knew the quickest way *exactly*. Victoria Station: Julia . . .

Julia didn't have a friend in the world except for Santay. The smooth surface of the station concourse might have been designed for him. He picked up speed.

Julia walked in a curious way, he thought as they approached each other. She was like a swan, her body gliding smoothly while she looked about, her legs paddling underneath her. He knew the kiss would be delivered right on the corner of his mouth.

As she bowed in front of him he wondered about the mysterious labyrinths of cloth swathed and buttoned round her body. He could only see her face and her ankles—she even wore gloves. Santay wanted to pass through the hangings of her wraparound skirt, draw aside any underthings, move through the darkness, and mingle there among her legs, admiring them; they would rise like a stand of pale trees, smelling of musk.

The two of them moved together to a table. They were always eager for the intelligent conspiracy of these meetings.

"So how is he?" asked Santay, carefully.

"He?" she asked, as though not knowing who he meant. "Oh, my husband. I don't think I've got one anymore. Not really." The faintest crop of a moustache hinted at some sexually devious trick that her mouth might possess.

"You've still got the piece of paper."

"Yes."

"Has it got worse?"

"Marriage is a funny thing," she replied. "It's not enough to have a store of good luck. It's talking, that's the problem. If you don't talk, you can't touch. Something so simple . . . I only talk with you."

"You're pretty poorly off," said Santay.

"That's not what I meant, you know . . ."

21

"I was joking," replied Santay, easily.

"I'm not just telling myself it's a mistake anymore. I'm dying in there. Each step he takes toward me is a cue for me to take a step in the opposite direction. We haven't seen each other's skin for a week."

"What will you do?"

"I don't know. You know what I'm most frightened of?"

"No."

"That I've wasted time."

"We're all doing that," replied Santay.

"And sex . . . God."

"What?"

"There's so much of it. Look at all these people. They've all got . . . every one of them has got . . ."

"Genitals."

"Yes. Secret genitals."

"Very secret. Pouches and bags and muscular rods of skin."

"So they're all at it," said Julia in disbelief, counting the streaming crowds. "Look at them all."

"You're one of them."

"Do I have to be?"

"Yes."

"Who are they? Are they all like me?"

They guessed, while passengers fled around them, what everyone did for a living. Talking in undertones they made snap judgments:

"Bricklayer, mum makes sandwiches."

"Sister, fourteen, annoys him. She wants to go out with his mates."

"Look. Middle manager, big shop somewhere."

"Hairdressing franchise in . . ."

"Selfridges?"

"Maybe." Santay nods his head.

Julia gathered herself for this. "It does mean, though," she admitted, "that I can't come here anymore."

"Why not?"

"I don't go by train anymore. I've left home."

"Ah . . ."

Santay felt (again) as though he was falling from a great height. (Always to land in the same chair.)

ON HIS RETURN Santay parked at the bottom of the three impossible steps. He was just beyond the cover of the porch, dampened by the drizzle, lobbing the cricket ball up against the door. He was sated by gossip, but anxious that the scrap of paper with Julia's temporary phone number on it was too fragile a link to last out. It was gone, wasn't it? It might drag its heels but it was over.

Molly was not answering. He knew she was in. He checked the street. Only two, no, three figures. One was looking at him, and worried, crossing the road to avoid. The other two were farther away. He threw the ball again, but it dropped and stayed at the top of the steps. He waited. Where was she?

Santay was interrupted by the arrival now of the figure who'd rocked from one foot to another in a slow amble toward him. The young man (with a moustache) stopped and asked if Santay wanted any help. He was standing with a very humble stance: his shoulders sloped down to relaxed hands and he leaned forward in a naturally trustful attitude.

"If you could just pull me up these three steps to the door," said Santay briskly, aware that he was couching his speech specifically: middle-aged unfortunate to younger, more fortunate person. He swiveled his chair to be ready for the stranger to tow him up backward. He felt the man take a grip, and calmed himself by fielding idle judgments about several figures hurrying into the mews opposite. Then he began to move. The stranger was suddenly disconcertingly intimate, too near . . . Santay heard several

23

half-complete sentences come in between other noises, like breathing and false half-grunts.

"Hup . . . ah . . . one . . . heave . . . two. Not so . . . hup . . . easy."

Santay thanked him when they reached the top, and prepared himself to say goodbye. There was a pause. What was happening behind? The man was rustling in his pockets. Was he going to give money? (Some people had been that ashamed.) The mews was empty, the darting figures had disappeared from the constricted perspective at the other end. Just at that moment it was surreally quiet on Chapel Street. Apart from a rich car serenely pressing on the wet tarmac in the next street, all Santay could hear was the faint roar in the background that he could easily think was the thrumming of the blood in his own head, but which was in fact made by the city's motors: traffic, air-conditioning, aeroplanes, subterranean trains. Behind him there was the familiar sound of the front-door lock turning.

Still facing backward he was hauled in, like a difficult bit of cheap furniture, like a strange find dragged home.

He said, "Ahh . . ." and tried to look over his shoulder. It was difficult to speak out. Who was this person? If he wasn't turned before traveling through the tunnel (the tied-up rubbish bags, boxes, and old split suitcases funneled tenants into the house), then at the other end there would be a problem. He had to be facing forward to go downstairs. The only place to turn without dislodging any of the precariously balanced structures on either side of the hallway was in the area left free for the door to operate.

Backward he passed the first door. (Closed. Where was Molly?) Then, outside Skim and Marek's door, they came to a halt.

"Hmm. Where d'you want to go?" The voice behind was in the flight path of Santay's ear, meaning that the man was standing down on the second or third step.

24

"Down to the landing, if possible. You'll have to take me back up to the door so we can turn round. Sorry."

"Wait . . . wait . . ."

Santay began an involuntary move backward as the man changed the grip of his hands. There was something sinister about the stranger's muttering to himself, and, because of his dead nerves and because the man's grip ended up being somewhere underneath the chair, he could no longer be sure of how he was being held, and this made Santay wonder if he wasn't beginning to float. He looked down at his physical messiness and thought, "None of this belongs to me." It didn't help that tilted backward in his chair with the stranger's chin pressing into his shoulder he found himself adopting the position of an astronaut. He resolutely kept looking forward to avoid the sudden nearness of the face. They struggled down with almost as much effort as if they'd been trying to go up the stairs.

The final bump was the landing, and the man stepped out from behind the controls.

Santay said, "This is my room. Thanks. I can manage from here."

"Right-ho," the stranger replied, his foreign accent changing this expression; coming from him it dropped softly, losing its usual pre-war briskness. He returned back up the few stairs to the hall, swinging from side to side on each elastic toehold, and then turned to his left and went through the second doorway.

So that was *Marek*.

Back in his own room Santay steered himself to the window. At the rear of the house the windows let out onto three sides of an inner yard the size of a parking space. The fourth side was the wall of the next-door house. Looking up you saw the small portion of sky; looking down you might have an aerial view of the landlady crawling slowly like a large black beetle, pulling down the soggy washing in such a way as to look like she was punishing it. By facing

25

toward the front of the house and looking slightly upward Santay could see into Skim and Marek's room.

Santay watched for Marek's shape to appear at the window. It didn't happen. Santay made several turns around his room, imagining at the same point of each turn (by the hard bed) the ghosts of Gabriella's legs in the air at the thought of this Marek.

He settled down to a regular wait, with the odd pigeon scattering over the cable-dissected patch of gray, the windowsills swelling again, getting heavily soaked with the afternoon drizzle, and the interminable lines of bricks—all this disappearing in the failed and mediocre daylight.

In the evening Marek appeared. His head occupied the bottom-center square of the window frame. That would mean he was seated at the table. One side of his face was lit by a flare of light that grew out of the left-hand corner; it was probably a bedside lamp. Santay charged the legs of his tripod and swapped the lens on the camera, exposing the film for several different numbers of seconds. It would be a good photo. He liked the idea that Marek's soul took such a long time to be imprinted onto the faultless memory of his film.

MRS. GORSE WATCHED as Hawkins unconcernedly circled the basket of washing which had returned to the kitchen. It meant nothing to him that it was sopping wet.

But these small annoyances were the most insistent! She'd had to learn to watch her own frustration from a distance; sometimes she'd even managed to laugh at how absurd many of her actions were, but even this would have been accompanied by great clouds of moodiness sliding along at different speeds. On Sunday, for instance, she'd go to market and there'd be a dress with dark flowers printed on it, which she would buy, thinking it to be for someone else. And her autobiography—not too long hence she'd be taking her typewriter back to the same market she'd bought it from, but at this very moment she was wasting Molly's time with that request for a search among the tins of photographs.

"Always a fight!" cried Mrs. Gorse. Hawkins looked alarmed, then just as quickly returned to his ordinary calm. Mrs. Gorse went and sat in her chair, the typewriter in front of her. "It is a fight," she said, "to serve the existing minute. Only the existing minute! And another thing. It gets worse as I get older."

Hawkins took no notice. There was nothing you could teach him about age. He'd had endless lives.

She told herself, "The washing is wet. So what? This is nothing! Nothing!"

To win perspective she reminded herself of just how far she'd gone, how much she'd endured, how many large events she'd tried but been unable to change. Since Time's interference with her, she could see all circumstances, either one by one, or all at once. She could take the beginning of the world and the end of the world and fold them together to wrap up every single moment—and then hold it up to the light and *mark* that one concentrated, blindingly colorful glimpse of *change,* yet she could not alter anything . . .

Not that she hadn't tried, she had, with all she possessed. To take a thousand bruises on the soles of her feet at a stroke, to shake with the accumulated voltage of all torture, to burn with an infinite number of war wounds, or ride with the orating tyrant's hand as it comes down again and again in condemnation of a race or a creed and be unable to haul it to a stop, to be unable to soothe one single argument—that was frustration! She'd seen her husband roped up and kneeling in the lineup, blindfolded like the others, and the firing squad cocking one knee to rest their rifles against the prisoners' backs . . .

The terror was that despite a seething sense of injustice she had been unable to inspire one single moment of deviation according to her will. She'd given up. In exhaustion! She was only human.

27

The washing getting wet was nothing in comparison, after all. How dare such a small thing stymie her.

She was worried. (The lines came down on her forehead.) This last phase of her life held unknown ... unknown what? Surprises?

"But I am desperate for a surprise," continued Mrs. Gorse, cheering up, speaking to Hawkins, "I haven't had one since puberty."

SIX

SKIM AND MAREK were sharing a room, but they hadn't met, not beyond a handshake and a hello. Their first meeting, their first proper confluence, had been delayed for a while because their routines differed.

Skim woke before Marek.

Getting up, he would look across and all that was visible of Marek was his hair, like a black mop stuck in a soft accident of pillows and assorted bedcovers. He'd pick up his work clothes from where they'd fallen round the edge of his bed and start the repeat pattern of his days in the semi-dark, dressing easily because the garments were permanently cramped to fit his shape, sure in his sorting of the buttons and the belt which he'd successfully hiked time after time.

Marek would continue to sleep, inventing on the surface of dreams in his clamp of sheets and pillows. He'd get up, finally, at some unknown hour, sitting for long minutes on the edge of his bed, recovering slowly, a casualty of sleep. He'd rescue some damaged-looking underclothes from somewhere, and then take more care over the garments that were going to be seen. In various parts of the room, resting,

29

deflated, never folded, were further victims: the tailcoat, a beret, a pair of black trousers with a stripe down the side. By the time Marek had hatched himself, midday had usually passed unnoticed.

Skim worked, whereas Marek didn't, so during the day they missed each other.

Skim disliked the early days of the autumn term. The new intake arrived, nervous like tourists. He had to do a series of facile demonstrations which involved the setting-up of each student's workbench. Their seats then filled up, tools were set waving clumsily in their hopeless hands, molds broke, soundtape splices fell apart. These sessions were a farce, mostly. Budding actors trying to change a plug! The fooling youths encouraged their debt to each other's humor. They regarded him as some sort of woodshed figure, but toward the end of term, when the shows were on, he would be indispensable.

When he returned to Chapel Street each evening he would be alone in the room—Marek was never there. After he'd dispatched his clothes to their usual position guarding the bed and climbed under the covers, he'd still be alone. The room grew quiet and dark, restful for him. Lying on his back, listening to the bump of people moving in the house, he'd think about eating; he'd run through a list of favorite chocolate products available from the late-night Italian place, the tiny shop that surprised newcomers to the mews opposite with its sudden retail advertising glued in the residential window.

By the time he got up to go to the shop, an hour or so later, blackness would have settled as close as it could on the energetic city, and he'd waste no time in getting back to bed, to lie there while he sucked and chewed, and then he'd wait (not long) for the glucose to sing in his blood and produce the passionate thoughts that would eventually exhaust him and carry him off in a sugary stupor to a strange but welcome frontier, where his mind slipped gracefully between the workshop, the student projects, his home, the landlady, his own opinion, final sleep.

Late at night Marek would be watched. Moving through the dreary horizons of those people who had territories in doorways, on benches and under arches, he was tracked, but never touched. His gait had an innocence to it, as though he might be walking hand in hand with a girl he was in love with, and was therefore to be left alone. In reality there was an angel who linked arms with him whenever he was in danger. Inside his head he would be sorting out love, and thinking of music. He would try his quietest to come in.

During weekends Skim avoided Marek. He pretended to be asleep until Marek dressed and went out. He would lie for hours and do nothing. He had no friends, and wondered where Marek went, why Marek had friends. He felt locked into his own cynical, unapproachable character. When he compared himself to Marek he had the sensation that he was hanging on by his nails but still falling, perceptibly falling. Then came the argument (following well-worn logic) that always discovered the same conclusion: he was glad to be imprisoned inside this character, his character, because it stopped him from falling for anything, neither love, nor religion, nor belief in humankind's greatness, nor any other infantile invention.

Gabriella had met both of them before they'd spoken to each other. She knew everyone in the house. Her cleaning took her into every room.

Some were more interesting than others. Claude, for instance, occupying the back room on the first floor, showed her photographs of his anthropological adventures. She'd seen him wearing a loin-strap and a painted face, but standing next to the other fit young bucks in the photo he'd looked like a leprechaun. Angelika Brown occupied the attic, which had a kitchenette attached. She was often away riding a horse across various different countries, but when she was there she treated Gabriella to a wild, sunny smile. Monsieur Villiers was a chef who stored a selection of antique cheeses under a glass dome. He hardly said a word to her, which always made her want to laugh. She felt like she ought to polish the glass dome. Clean, clean, clean. She agreed with the notes taped by Mrs. Gorse to the walls of the bathrooms and lavatories:

PLEASE. THIS BATHROOM IS NOT LIKE IN A HOTEL. IF THERE IS DIRT HERE IT IS YOURS. GET RID OF IT. IF SOMETHING DOESN'T WORK IT IS YOUR FAULT. MEND IT. I AM NOT HERE ON THIS EARTH TO MEND YOUR TOILETS AND YOUR TAPS.

The notes were the dirtiest, tattiest things in the house. Gabriella was not sure about the deal she'd made. How much did cleaners get paid in this country? She did sums in her head while she worked. So much an hour; rent equals this much; but then she had a room to herself; but it was in the basement . . . The basement. Soon she would have a visitor there as well. This was causing her anxiety. She told herself not to fret. "Keep your mouth shut. Don' worry what *they* think."

"They." She had already lumped the two of them together. Skim and Marek.

It happened at the end of a long, slow London Sunday. Marek was woken up very early that morning by Molly, her utilitarian architecture shrouded in a winceyette nightgown, who told him that there was a friend of his waiting at the front door. Marek left the room wearing a T-shirt and a towel, and came back with a stranger. They were whispering keenly.

Skim was awake, but pretended to be asleep. He listened to the muted noises of friendship—they sounded like birds crooning for food—and when he opened a fraction of an eye he saw through the blurred vibration of its lashes a rucksack swinging from the shoulder of a tall young man.

He shut his eye again and listened to the sound of rummaging. The easy slip of plastic clothes was familiar to him. Marek's cry of excitement? Then there was the light slap of some object being put down on his worktable underneath the window, and more whispering while Marek got dressed. They left the room. Skim went back to sleep.

Later he awoke not knowing where he was. This put an immediate cramp of unhappiness onto the start of the day, and even though he quickly recognized the room, and himself, he had to go far back along his own personal history as a matter of course in order to recover. He became preoccupied with finding if there were any markers, any fixed events that prescribed his . . . his what? What was he stuck with? A point of view? A mentality? Or was it all character? Why, he asked himself, throwing back the bedclothes and flexing the soreness in his body, why would he always choose to scoff, not just at religion, but anything? Was it because of his determination to find out how things physically, practically, worked?

Looking down he saw the chips of skin missing from his hands. The disproportionate irritation these small wounds caused! Beneath his hands, on the table by the window, lay two handsomely wrapped slabs: Swiss praline with nuts. Serious chocolate. They looked strangely new and shiny in the drab room, and without hesitation Skim recalled the easy, generous nature of his roommate. He knew that Marek had lent clothes and scraps of money to Gabriella without even asking for them back. It was obvious that he, Skim, could take a square of chocolate, or even, he decided as the silver paper tore erratically from around the nut-encrusted surface, a whole line.

There was, thought Skim as he walked up and down, something, a dichotomy in his character, an inner tangle that was difficult to puzzle out. On the one hand he had this dreary cynical mentality or viewpoint. He respected no one, there was no job that wasn't meaningless, no effort that

33

wasn't endlessly unsatisfying. Yet he had this bloody *energy*! If only he had either one without the other, he could be a wholly true, correctly tuned character, at peace with himself. He remembered the surprising depth of loathing he had felt at the sight of the Hare Krishnas dancing through the underground station in their absurd outfits, the sound of their instruments maddeningly amplified by the tunnel and aimed directly at him, the only person approaching from the opposite direction. But then the last of them to walk by had been a silent boy, his shaven head tilted forward, who'd moved past with a floating equilibrium, so easy a sight that Skim had wanted to turn and call out a question—any question.

Arriving back at the chocolate, he remembered hearing the hands of the visitor unpacking it from the rucksack. It seemed a long time ago. He wondered where they'd gone. Without worrying about it too much he took another finger of the nut praline.

Sitting down, but restless, he judged himself as being a vessel containing two equal but opposing forces. It became, then, a bleak view: it meant he was tearing himself apart. The tightness of recent sleep across his chest seemed to validate the conclusion. His energy pulled against his cynicism, just as the drive-force would always struggle against the drag coefficient; there was lift, but at the same time there was the terrible weight of gravity; plus was always stopped by minus. There was a pitilessly cruel reasoning behind the design of this world, he thought, and yet nobody could accuse God of not being careful: it was made up of such an extravagant and exact logic. He found that he was holding his breath, sitting on his bed, catastrophically bogged down. The pessimism ate into him, but there was nowhere he could go until he'd tipped himself out of the stalemate one way or the other.

He saw, with a twinge of guilt, that he had finished off one of the Swiss slabs, but there was still one left. It was in a way better that he'd eaten a whole one because he'd now have to go out and buy another to replace it.

He idled for the rest of the day. There was no one for him to visit. Anyone he thought of he denounced as being not worth it. He started instead on a prop for a spoof horror show, a picture to be made out of soft clay so that when The Beast came and caused a blackout a stagehand could take it off the wall and mulch it into an absurd shape.

Being unable to cope with a day off was a depressing notion. The hours were ticked off against nothing, marked just by themselves, and the rise and fade of light.

MAREK HAD A very different prelude to the first real meeting between the two of them which was to happen in the evening of that Sunday. The visitor from abroad was a virtual stranger. In fact when Marek had first seen the wildly happy face under the yellow bulb in the hallway he didn't know who it was, only that it was someone who obviously knew *him* because this figure was advancing with open arms down the corridor of old junk, rucksack bumping against the twin walls of unsorted material for the landlady's autobiography. Marek had his hand shaken.

"Hello!" Marek exclaimed.

"Hello," said the visitor, with the fervor of someone who has had a terrible journey and doesn't know what he's doing there anyway.

"Who are you?" asked Marek, recklessly.

"What?" The stranger was suddenly uncertain, more at sea than he had been on the ferry.

"I don't know who you are," said Marek, and laughed. "I don't, really, I don't."

"Federico! You remember!"

"Federico?"

"The brother of Maria . . . don't you remember, in Spain?"

35

"Ah, Maria! Yes of course, Federico the brother of Maria!"

"Hello!"

"Hello! You must come in. Or we'll go for breakfast. There's someone asleep . . ."

They tiptoed in.

"Look, look what I have for you," whispered Federico, as he unpacked his rucksack, rubbed with strangeness at being in a room with a sleeping man in the middle of a foreign city. He withdrew an envelope. "The money. The money for your music course. It turned up!"

"Ah!" cried Marek, taking the envelope and holding it in both hands.

"And you like chocolate?"

Federico put down two slabs.

Marek led the way out of the house. He hadn't a clue where they could go. His metronomic gait had at one time or another covered most of central London on foot. After a while he remembered a café behind Regent Street that never locked its doors.

Next to him Federico the visitor struggled with words. He was tall, a disconnected, gangling man who several times bumped into Marek as they walked side by side. Marek had already written off the morning. This Federico had come along with the money. He must be looked after!

He could pay his music fees. So, all the sounds gathered by his ears were used. Federico's voice came down at him from one side. Marek recognized the strain, how the voice struggled to move through the vowels. Every sentence that managed to get past his uncooperative mouth was rewarded with an exclamation mark at the end of it. Marek himself had learned English from a different direction, but none the less he was familiar with this mangled growling. The fingers of his left hand curled and uncurled. He would try and describe the voice. His footfalls counted the rhythm. His left hand formed a shape and swam through

36

the air in an imitation of a separate animal, pulsing and twisting to follow the contours of Federico's voice. With his right hand he used other sounds that came to him on this early Sunday-morning walk: the winding of a builder's crane, the jump and rattle of a taxi driving over a pothole, the break of a pigeon's wings. Surreptitiously Marek treated the causality of the world as an intentional, ordered symphony. "My head," thought Marek, "should be always like this, a ball-shaped microphone."

In the café (which was open and about to take, well, only a small bit of the money) Marek began to talk about the things that the visitor ought to do in London. The walk along the river, the free disco, the discount college bars and cafés, the sights of bridges and buildings, and the individual treasures in various galleries and other locations. For particular objects Marek had a special affection, he had the feeling that they were his friends. There was a Moroccan shop fitting in Piccadilly that gonged when the door was opened. The old London buses. Big Ben itself. He had listened in all these places.

It wasn't until the early evening that he found himself able to wander home. Federico had been introduced to some other friends and he'd been settled into a hostel for a very reasonable rent (although he'd had to lend him enough for the month in advance). But Marek was now free.

There was something he liked about walking by himself through the streets. His most productive ideas came to him then, suddenly bursting like magic out of the run-of-the-mill production of ordinary thoughts. Occasionally he would mutter "Yes!" in gratitude at such a flooding of mental excitement, and he would follow up with work: a humming percussion perhaps.

But mostly he thought of women. He didn't think about their bodies, or what he could possibly do to them to convince them of his seductiveness. He thought about their faces, their eyes, their smiles. Their best expressions danced

37

in front of him as he walked, one switching for another like lanterns. Magical femininity held a sway over him, and he rejoiced in it. Women recognized this and stuck like magnets. He had slept with none of them. He was going to wait.

When Marek got back to his room Skim was there. Embarrassment gathered in the room like a chemical they produced when their two figures were mixed together. They so rarely saw each other up and dressed and expecting comment. Skim loomed, bulky, larger than life; he was standing by the table under the window with a contorted face.

"I have a confession to make . . ." he began. Marek turned toward him in a friendly enquiry. Feeling already a little browbeaten, he was ready now for some minor bad news—a problem with the room, or something lost.

"I've eaten your chocolate," said Skim.

"What?"

"I've got the covers," said Skim, smoothing the printed wrappers onto the table, "so I can go tomorrow and buy them again."

Marek went up to the table and looked down at the wrappers. He picked one up by the corner.

"Nut praline," he said, looking at Skim with a blank expression.

"I forgot it was Sunday. I was going to replace them, and then I realized . . ." said Skim, beginning to laugh. Marek looked so comical with that moustache twitching. He felt quite sick with chocolate.

"I don't believe it," said Marek, acting a bleak disappointment. "You have stolen it."

Skim wasn't quite sure. Was he angry?

Marek's return laugh was like a hand on the small of his back, gathering him, holding him up.

SEVEN

Mrs. Gorse barged through the door as though it was a personal affront to her passage. When she was in the room she raised a fist to give the door a perfunctory rap, a punishment for being in the way. She stood, breathing heavily through a small round mouth, and quickly gave the place a worried once-over, checking for breakages or secrets. After a brief bout of blinking she turned to Skim.

"Skim!"

"Yes Mrs. Gorse."

"I don't want any more trouble with Gabriella."

"What trouble?"

"She has got her boy coming to stay here in my house. God knows I allow that."

"There's no trouble with me . . ."

"Sex and love," said Mrs. Gorse, getting into the stride of a major speech, "sex and love, they used to be the same thing. The very same! Like that!" She clapped her hands together. "Now they are different. Now they are cut in half. I heard on the radio this afternoon 'vagrancy sex.' Vagrancy? What does this mean? Everyone is turning into tramps? Skim, watch out, you will have the soul of a tramp, with your vagrancy sex and your cutting of love and sex away from each other!"

She nodded at him, smiling and grimacing and at the same time turning to go. Her last words rang out as though she could see a heavy weight swinging toward him: "Watch out!" she said.

"Mrs. Gorse . . ." began Skim, but she'd gone.

EIGHT

GABRIELLA WORKED TWO days a week. She changed the sheets and shook a duster at people's rooms on Mondays; on Fridays she swished a cloth round the bathrooms and raked the stairs with a brush.

She was unhappy with her basement room. The weight of the house was bearing down on the ceiling—the fact that none of the doors closed in the basement was proof that it was too heavy. She used the wastepaper basket to prop her door more or less against the jamb. "These rooms were never designed to be lived in, anyway," she thought. Hers should have been a workshop; a washing room should have been in Mrs. Gorse's kitchen; a shower had been squeezed in with the toilet; the coal cellar was now the larder.

She had her worries, too, pinning her down. There was a pile of old, old memories that she had to walk round with, all decorated with fancy Catholic words, shrouded in a Latin mist.

Words stayed on for ever. They were as heavy as iron. "Mortal Sin." She'd love to kill someone and get the thing irrevocably over and done with, but she was still stuck on Venial Sin, which had to be humored; she moved along its scale of punishment, balancing her behavior against its demands, in order to prevent it from tilting her into damnation. Why couldn't she get rid of it? That was the challenge she thought she would never get out from underneath: the search for a remnant of herself that could be distilled to another place, away from all these ideas, these words.

She didn't have enough time to think about all this. She flew from one interruption to the next, following Mrs. Gorse's voice. She wished she could live in a place where each thought would come from her and belong to her.

No chance. The basement was a furious hive of character. Two short-term tenants chattered and bumped in the room next to hers. Mrs. Gorse was almost permanently resident in the crowded kitchen, digging about in her racks of old vegetables or assaulting, in bursts, the typewriter. Gabriella could only try to guard her little space for herself and try to work out her complex sexual feelings.

The best rooms taunted her. If she could move here, upstairs, she would be happier. The graceful tall windows invited you to walk through to however far a horizon was on offer; the large doors welcomed you; the impressive cornicing, although only dimly visible, imparted a stately quality to the walk up the stairs—then, because of the grand proportions, the airiness of the place, you were always looking upward, so you could ignore the tea and butter that had been rubbed into the threadbare rugs and carpets. On every landing there was the peaceful bulk of resting furniture. She'd thrive in this atmosphere—listen: the grandmother clock, as always, but such quiet, you could hear a toe caught in a torn sheet.

Unfortunately it was unlikely she'd ever get to move in up here. It had been colonized by the more permanent tenants, those who had been rewarded for good behavior and honorable payment of rent.

Claude stepped out of his room and beckoned her.

42

She followed, closing in on his incomprehensible whisper, allowing him to guide her into his room. He checked the stairwell and closed the door behind him softly as though the building would fall if he was not so careful.

"Why does it always happen to me?" he asked, his eyes baldly popping.

"What?" enquired Gabriella.

"I'm not a difficult or nosy tenant am I?" Claude knew he wasn't.

"I don' think so," replied Gabriella.

"I've got something to show you," he said. "Sit down, sit down."

Gabriella perched on his bed. He turned away from her and sank to his knees by the table—she wondered what it would be. More photographs? He was organizing an exhibition of his travels. He'd moved through some of the world's most hair-raising conflict zones without any harm coming to him. No one had noticed he was there. Bullets passed straight through him without even pausing.

He was tugging at a large metal box hidden by a rug under the table. Gabriella speculated on his rear. It was impossible to picture him kneeling over Molly like that. Both pairs of corduroys in a heap on the floor! She didn't see how they could have mated. It was absurd. What did they talk about?

"This is really something, look," said Claude, his insect's legs buckling under the weight before he could put it down at her feet. He opened the lid and took out a flat wooden box, the size of a jewelry case, and then dipped his other hand in to fetch one of many large Victorian volumes dressed in leather which looked as though they'd slumbered together in the bottom of the trunk for years.

"First," said Claude, putting the wooden box on Gabriella's lap. He was waiting for her to open it.

Reclining snugly in a molded interior lined with blue velvet was an old, crudely constructed pistol. It had an ivory handle. Pegged in a neatly drilled compartment beside the barrel were a dozen rounds of ammunition. Gabriella unplugged one. The bullet looked suspicious, the joint between the lead and the brass bubbled with some leaked crystalline substance.

"And," said Claude, lifting the pistol, indicating an inscription on the handle. She read MAJOR L. J. W. GORSE.

"*Mr.* Gorse?" she suggested.

"I would think it must be before that—maybe his father. Do you know anything about him?"

"No I don' . . ."

Claude moaned, "Why does it always happen to me?" He was weighing the revolver, giving the impression of being used to handling such a thing. Guns? Yes, he'd taken quite a few away from people who couldn't be trusted to behave.

"Obviously I don't want this lot in my room. It's live ammunition," he continued, adopting now a professional tone, "and highly unstable."

Gabriella imagined that the bullet in her hand might pop, so she put it back. The whole box might explode. She closed the lid and handed it back to him.

"It's got to be disposed of, I suppose," said Claude wearily.

"I tell Mrs. Gorse," said Gabriella, gathering her safe dusters and cleaning fluids again.

"No, no no," said Claude, "I thought of that, but then she'd accuse me, wouldn't she, of prying. If she wants to hide the gun . . ."

"Where you found it?"

Claude turned his oversize nose and aimed it at the fireplace. "Behind there," he said. "I levered the board off because I thought I might use a real fire, just once in a while, every now and again. But I wouldn't want Mrs. Gorse to know I'd done that."

Gabriella felt a flurry of annoyance: Claude was scared

44

of Mrs. Gorse. "I ask Santay," she said. "He'll know what to do. He's her favorite." She was ready to leave.

Claude lugged the box back to the table, his feet shuffling to avoid damage to his shins.

"Why does it always happen to me, eh?" asked Claude with satisfaction.

"I don' know," said Gabriella. "Muss be your character. Exciting. Lots of adventure."

"No," said Claude earnestly, "no, I'm sure not. I hate violence, I *hate* it, and now it's here in the room, you know, with me."

Gabriella exchanged goodbyes with him and left. She continued working her way up the stairs, hoping not to see anyone else.

Some of them up here were peculiarly, sadly old, and the passive touch of the house imparted no style of romance to them as it did to the shining young. The old ones were not so afraid of Mrs. Gorse, though—they were used to her, they didn't mind that she behaved like a large and out-of-control spy, bursting into their rooms in an explosion of commands and questions.

Yes, Mrs. Gorse had perfected the art of not knocking. Although she was such a size and weight, and despite misleading evidence (the power of her voice, the amount of noise she made once she was in the room), she moved along the passages and up and down the stairs with a supernatural quietness. The slower gents had been caught out. When she saw them hopping with one foot entangled in a pair of underpants she would retreat, saying in a short, urgent way, "Oop-lah."

How had Mrs. Gorse been born? Gabriella could see Marek pointing and Skim explaining in a serious tone. They had made up several stories. She had listened eagerly. Marek had settled on the idea that Mrs. Gorse had been found in the bottom of the decrepit metal bucket which always stood unused out in the corner of the little backyard, filling up with

45

rainwater when it was wet, emptying in the sun to reveal a distillation of black sediment. She'd either floated out of the bucket after a storm, as a seedling, and had grown to such monstrous proportions in the boiler room having been carried in on the bottom of someone's shoe, or she'd crawled out of the bucket in caterpillar form and had been trying to pupate ever since.

Gabriella smiled, remembering Marek's open laugh. Those two—a real pair. And she might want to include herself—a real trio. There was something about them. She carried the smile as she cleaned and cleaned.

NINE

◔❦◔

S<small>KIM AND</small> M<small>AREK</small> were due to become closer. A series of
incidents would add up to an unlikely intimacy. Skim, for
instance, was used to the brief disturbance caused by
Marek's coming in and trying to be quieter than the passing
of the night (failing only by a small, forgivable amount) but
on one occasion he stayed awake because of a peculiar
sight.

Marek had come in still smarting from some late night
rendezvous with the American girl or perhaps the French
girl Martine. He was sitting in the dark on the edge of his
bed, and at first Skim thought that he was having a fit. His
pale body was rocking back and forth, the hair showing
like patches of shadow in the gloom, and his hands were
floating in the air as though holding invisible ropes. Sometimes there were downward thrusts on the ropes, mysteriously violent, and followed by a manic energy that seized
his slim frame: he seemed spastic. His head was either
tipped downward so that his chin bumped on his chest, or
flung backward to expose the workings of the arteries and
windpipe, dipping in and out of the magical light reflected
by the increscent moon which hung close by, just outside

the window. Skim stared hard to get himself clear of sleep. He thought something had gone wrong with Marek. Was it grief? From his first stirring through to this state of alarm at his friend's behavior could only have taken a number of seconds, but when he realized what the answer was the sudden onset of alertness, of fearfulness, wasn't dissolved. He saw the glint of steel curved in Marek's hair, and heard a faint buzzing, and realized that Marek was listening to music.

Music . . . Skim continued to watch, not without a measure of embarrassment at the naked commitment. Marek's face, secure in its privacy, was alternately tightening along its lines, and then relaxing, the expression falling loose. His concentration was blanked off from anything else, severely intent on following the sound; it traveled into his ear, displaying its pattern of emphasis, its intricate, mathematical arrangement of time.

Skim saw Marek through to the end of this apparently tormenting experience. When the waspish sound in the earphones stopped, Marek slumped backward onto the bed. After a while he undressed slowly, discarding things piece by piece, and crawled into bed, making a hole for himself.

Skim wished for such an enthusiasm, a peg (with his name on it) that he could hang himself up on. In comparison to Marek he was fallen, he'd stopped in his life's tracks; it was left to him only to look enviously at someone so possessed . . .

When had he ever experienced *any* passion?

There had been some random occasions. Standing on a motorway bridge once, steaming in the rain, with the traffic pouring and sizzling underneath, he'd felt unaccountably moved by a force major to himself. Then there was that sighting of the disintegrated man lying on the street which had made him cry, but he'd known there was an evil showing-off in the tears. There had been other times, when he'd got himself into cheap and predictable situations: alone with a shamelessly sentimental TV program and a can of lager; moving among a large crowd having been alone in a room for days on end. These occasions had suddenly announced themselves without any warning, and they hadn't left any clue as to a logical pattern. They either made him feel miraculously small and insignificant, or special, chosen among men to experience this. But it would jar if he tried to reveal such incidents, or talk about them in an abstract way, because they'd be meaningless to anyone else's ear. Besides, they seemed bogus even to him. They added up to nothing, they were flaky.

Marek, it seemed, had found something that could switch it on for him: the button on the tape machine.

It made Skim angry.

He'd always avenged himself by despising life's fastenings, the ones that other people had found or invented for themselves, but despite himself he wanted to try and share what Marek had. The following evening gave him an opportunity.

Marek had found an unconventional use for the paper that he wrote his music on. The house, although it was bluffing with its façade (which by law had to be redecorated every three years), was brutally frank about its sad state of disrepair inside. Stains moved across the walls, cracks grinned, tiny, crookedly, between the windows, and the doors in the basement didn't shut anymore so they stood openly stating their case with loud drafts of air. In Skim and Marek's room a fringe of discoloration followed the seam between the ceiling and the wall above the window.

Marek stood on the beds and the table and sellotaped a copy of his first symphony over the top of it.

"That's not music," said Skim.

"Oh but yes," replied Marek, "it is the first part of writing music."

"But there's no notes."

49

"No, look, it is possible not to be so very exact at the start. Each line is an instrument, and you use symbols to describe what is happening. This is an earthquake; here an electric shock which turns into one long noise; it doesn't matter what note it is but it must go on to here—and so on. There is more potential of life. The musicians can improvise, the conductor also. Then afterward, maybe, if you need to, you can use notation. But there is so much that can happen outside of rhythm. Maybe you bring it back in later, whatever."

Skim asked if he could listen to the tape.

"Which one?" said Marek.

"I saw you with it last night. It looked good," replied Skim. He felt a surprising insecurity as he was speaking, a loss of confidence because of his jealousy.

Marek was looking about, prodding with his foot in his half of the room. The tape could have been anywhere. "This one," he said, picking one up off the table. "I've been listening to this one a lot recently." He handed it to Skim, who felt a prickle of disgust at the title: *Vesperi 1610.*

"Bloody hell," Skim said.

"What?" asked Marek, puzzled.

"Religious rubbish. Pompous turd-burglars, all priests are."

Skim dropped onto the bed and welcomed the usual calmness, the release that he always enjoyed after indulging in an insult.

"No no," said Marek, "idiot, it's just music."

A reprimand . . . Yes, Skim thought, he was being too serious about it. Just music. Maybe he should just listen.

TEN

SKIM AND MAREK'S room, unknown to its two occupants, had become an arena for Gabriella's working-out of an annoying conundrum in her sexual game-play.

She didn't particularly mind, for herself, that she was a virgin, although she did care desperately that no one should find out. It was the reason behind *why* she was a virgin, that was the real dilemma. It was something she had come to think of as a *kink*. If she could find her way out of it, this circular argument that enclosed her, then she wouldn't be a virgin for long.

It was a very cleverly cut cleft stick: she only ever wanted a man if she was frightened of him, but then she was frightened of him so . . . she ran away. This effectively ruled out any possibility of her being anything else but a virgin for the rest of her life.

She visited their room in order to get on with the crisis.

Nine-forty-five p.m. Marek had been thinking of something to do on the following day, perhaps some walk somewhere, or someone to visit. He was making fewer appointments in the evenings now that he felt comfortable being in the same room as this youth Skim with the damaged hands.

Skim had just finished some ice cream and had let the carton dangle down by the side of the bed until it touched the floor; then he'd let it drop. He liked the coldness in his throat.

When she tiptoed in.

There was Skim, dangerous, with his large body in bed, and a glare in his eye, and stiff hair that curled like metal springs; and there was Marek, not frightening enough. But she wanted to be in love with Marek. She loved his character, his charm. She wanted him in every way, it was just the kink that she had to iron out. He wasn't frightening enough. Maybe she could frighten herself.

They were both lying in bed fully dressed because it was cold. She crept across the room to Marek's bed and got in between the sheets.

"Cor blimey." Marek sometimes adopted an antique persona when speaking English. Gabriella smiled and took him in her arms. Marek peered out from the hook of her elbow.

"Shall I go?" asked Skim, a slow fury beginning because he was being put in an uncomfortable position. He blamed Gabriella.

"No," said Marek.

"No," repeated Gabriella, turning to look at him.

"He must not go," said Marek to Gabriella, only inches from her face, "he is my friend."

Although Skim felt the simplistic childishness of this remark (from someone who'd only known him a month or so, after all), nevertheless the prickle of the gooseberry was subsiding, he noticed. He was willing, nearly happy, to accept the calming effect on his temper, but he wasn't fooled. He wasn't going to be taken in by any nebulous idea of friendship being the normal state of affairs between humans who weren't starving.

The three of them became at ease together.

Gabriella started to pester Marek. He was super-conscious of where her hands were: one on his shoulder, the other on the back of his head.

Later Marek was explaining something to Gabriella.

"I don't believe in it," he said.

"Why not?" asked Gabriella, saying it as though it were a complaint, dragging his hair in her fingers.

"It's just that it's not right."

"It iz right."

"It's that thing of respect," said Marek.

Marek felt respect for almost anything living. Animals were easy: they had an unimpeachable honor, an incorruptible sincerity. If a human being didn't deserve respect he felt the sadness himself, and saw it only as a momentary lapse needing a touch of good luck to make the natural order of things spring back into position.

"What respect?" asked Gabriella in horror. "Don' you respect me?"

"Oh yes, utterly ... You are respectable—but I mean respect for yourself, for your own body. You shouldn't use it like a ... like a toffee to give away easily, because, if you do, when you really do want to give it away, you'll find it's gone already. No more toffees left."

"You mean to say," bluffed Gabriella, in wonder at the idea that she might ever be able to give her body to anyone, "no sex before marriage?" She turned to Skim. "Skim, help! No sex before marriage!"

"No marriage, before, during, or after sex," replied Skim.

Gabriella felt a thrill of danger. Her temperature rose. With her hands on one man she was swimming in the eyeline of the other.

Marek's voice interrupted.

"No, no, crikey," he said, urgently. "It's nothing to do with marriage."

She stopped stroking the back of his neck. "What is it then?" she asked.

"Love. It's to do with love. You must follow your heart and your spirit, not your body . . ."

They talked on. Skim began to doze, listening to them repeating their arguments. He decided not to answer when Gabriella called out to him to ask if he was still awake. Their voices dropped to a murmur to allow him peace, and his limbs bore heavier. Their words became disconnected from the setting, and came to him vaguely from a great distance. He remembered the comfort of adult voices floating toward him through his sleep when he was a child.

He heard Gabriella say, *voce velata*, "So, you do 'ave a spirit, then?"

Marek murmured a reply: "Yes." He sounded confident.

"Where is it?"

After thinking for a while Marek said, "It's inside my body . . ." He left the end of the sentence hanging high—it was obvious that he was about to say something else.

"Yes," encouraged Gabriella.

"But it wants to get out . . ." said Marek.

The words lasted for a long time among Skim's slumbering thoughts. "It wants to get out . . ."

He found himself obliged to follow a lazily developing scenario in his head. He was picking up a Bible, but it was a different Bible in this place he was in. It was sensible, it was modest, it was real—also smaller than usual, and delicate with extreme age. The cover was of stiff leather with strange symbols on the front (academics were still struggling with the scription). There were only three pages, made out of heavy cloth. He turned to the first page. There was just one line written in ink that was almost unreadable, it had been so faded by the smoothing against the words of so many people's thumbs. "You do have a spirit."

He turned to the next page.

54

"It's inside your body . . ."

He found himself agreeing. A movement of humility drugged him in his dream. He turned to the final page.

"But it wants to get out."

He ached with consentience.

Then there was the hard back cover which he turned to close the book.

Where was he?

Of course—a bed-and-breakfast place. There were always Bibles in the bedside tables. He had himself wander about in the strange room. Opening a cheap drawer, he replaced the ancient book. None had ever been stolen. How had they been distributed to all the B-and-Bs? Each one inscribed by hand. It was thought that God had written them himself . . .

He slept.

THE FOLLOWING MORNING Skim found that he'd woken late for work—it was the first time since he didn't know when. While he dressed Gabriella stirred. She was rumpled, still in her clothes. She gave Skim a sly look as she hurried from the room, only half awake.

He continued to dress, reluctantly. He hadn't wanted to wake up. There was nothing to get out of bed *for*. Everything looked miserably small. The table, the bed. His socks, for God's sake. His stomach twanged with hunger (a small automatic desire).

He wished for something larger than himself, that would subsume him, that required him to exist, something that he believed in enough, more than enough, or maybe something that believed in *him*. He wanted to give his wretched meandering freedom away.

The tape was there, on the table. *Vesperi 1610*—it looked remote, too clever with that Latin title and the cherub design on the cover. And it wasn't his, it was Marek's. To Skim it would be meaningless.

He got ready to go to work.

WHEN MAREK SURFACED he found himself alone. Everything was quiet, the stillness waiting for any slight noise that he might make. He was glad that Gabriella and Skim weren't there; he didn't feel like making any sort of effort.

He found himself wondering why he wasn't in love with Gabriella. Was it because she was trying to throw herself at him? He didn't think so. She was pretty, beautiful. Her eyebrows . . . He sometimes wondered if he would fall in love with someone if they had some sort of physical damage. He thought about Santay. Could he fall in love with a cripple? Yes. Nodding to himself as he sat on the edge of the bed, he followed along a list of disabilities with no problem until he reached damaged eyes and there, he thought, he might have to draw a line, he couldn't work out why. Gabriella, however, was very pretty; he could remember her hands as though they were still on him. He had reveled in that one stroking his hair. The memory brushed his nape pleasurably (he was reminded of Hawkins's rising action when he was stroked along his humped back). But he wasn't in love with Gabriella. Probably, he mused, absently looking round for his address book, because he was still in love with those other two girls.

He flipped through the pages and found Martine's name. She was so beautiful, even her name was beautiful. (But she wasn't as *pretty* as Gabriella; Marek had run the two words—"pretty" and "beautiful"—so often through his thinking that they had quite separate tracks.) He would phone Martine now and visit her.

While he searched for his bag of money he was aware of a vague worry: why did he love so many women? It felt irresponsible, but he had to admit it was true he felt the

56

same shift of excitement when he was with either Martine, or Kate . . .

(His purse was empty. Why did he have a purse? It was always empty. Every time he found it it had nothing in it except a slight hope which escaped, it evaporated when he pulled back the zip.) Last week there had been that American girl with the long, thin arms and the ripped T-shirts. Why did he no longer love her? It was a puzzle, and he didn't know the answer. The fact that he was confused didn't frighten or weary him—he accepted it because he foresaw that when he really fell in love with someone there would be a sign of some sort. He would *know*, and the proof would stay. The love would stay. He wouldn't be able to get rid of it. It would be real, as real as stone in his heart. Thinking about it made his chest swell unbearably until tears sprang from his eyes; Martine's address and telephone number blurred on the page in front of him. Maybe Martine would be the one. He knew her number off by heart. He caught at the English phrase "off by heart." Perhaps this was a sign.

After his phone call he returned to the room and his eye was caught by the tape. He remembered Skim asking for and then rejecting it. Idly he picked it up and turned it in his hands. The plastic box was worn out—it opened with tell-tale ease. How incredible that such music should be encoded on this thin, insubstantial stuff, played in greater splendor, to more people, than when it was first composed almost four hundred years ago.

He recognized that he'd finished with it, though. He'd chased it to death, loving every turn.

He had an idea, and began to assemble paper and scissors.

So when Skim returned he found a small square parcel lying on his pillow.

A gift. This was serious. Because Skim enjoyed disliking

people. Finding fault formulae in anyone he met had always been a challenge. He could usually give a damning critique after the first few minutes of a meeting. For his own amusement he'd consciously developed the speed of this faculty. He'd become so fast that if he was told about a person in advance he would make several strategic guesses as a standard preparation for meeting them. The nastier those judgments were the more he wanted to see the person face to face and prove himself right. Then he could get them underfoot in seconds flat.

He unwrapped the small parcel. There was a mass of color—an explosive modern design in felt-tip pen. The tape had a new, homemade title. He read, GROOVY SOUNDS BY MONTEVERDI.

He saw the Walkman had been left there for him. As he put the earphones on and inserted the tape he was caused to remember the sight that was associated with it: Marek's ethereal conducting of the piece. He lay on his bed and listened, seeing in his mind's eye Marek's shadowy body waving like a tree under a windy sky. At the moment he couldn't quite see the attraction with this boys' chorus wailing in his ear. But perhaps he ought to force himself. His memory of Marek was evidence of what music must be, of what it could do: that it worked as a tool for tuning one's emotions to make them sing in time. Yes. He enjoyed thinking of music as something practical, a tool designed on purpose for a specific job. He just needed to practice using it enough.

ELEVEN

◆

Mrs. Gorse levered the meat from the tin onto Hawkins's plate. It was one of the few things that made him break out into a trot across the kitchen floor.

With difficulty she regained the upright position. "You are to be quiet now. No more bothering me for your dinner. This is important. I need peace and quiet. Enjoy it. Go on." Hawkins scouted for a starting point, his nose bumping gently over the surface of the jellied meat.

She made herself tea. She sharpened her pencil and cleared a reasonable space around her typewriter. After looking around, checking to see whether there would be anything else that might interrupt her, she sat down, and breathed three deep breaths. This would be the beginning of a new attitude to her work. She must cultivate self-discipline. A brain like hers was not suited for an autobiography. Not that there was any shortage of material. In addition to her time-less world knowledge she had a personal encyclopedia—the names of people, of places, the dates of personal and political events, the characters of artists, politicians, and journalists she had known—but she was so humming with the myriad complications of her intuition that having snatched at a sequence of real memory she was liable to be picked up and carried off to anywhere, anytime. She must try and forget that she had up until this moment only ever made a random connection with her typewriter.

Breaking through the distilled quietness of her basement kitchen, she began poking at the machine:

> *Children now, they have a sick pigeon in a cardboard box, and they feed it porridge, but I had a man, a grown man, injured. I was alone, you understand, on the streets, there was a war going on, and death like yet another bloody bloody enemy. We hid together, my soldier and I, it was in a railway tunnel. He was a Communist of course so he wore glasses.*
>
> *I scrounged for us. He had gangrene but I didn't know it as far as I knew all men smelt like that.*
>
> *There was nothing odd about my intuition you see. Not to me. Understand at that time my efforts to see and hear in all directions at once. Understand that when Time chose me to interfere with, I thought that's what happened to everyone. But not for long. My God no not for long!*
>
> *When my soldier died I went out into the daylight again, I went back to the deserted cloth factory. I knew puberty was coming. I counted the little hairs as they arrived, I pinched my breasts. I watched animals, I knew I was in for a shocking time. But I was not prepared for what happened.*

She paused. The accusation flashed: Mad! She's mad, that old lady.

60

One day she would denounce herself like that.

Her hand hovered like an antique claw over the type-writer. How could she put it, the way this thing had grown like a different person in her?

Her first sexual stirring had been like a small animal turning in its bed. But then she'd found that her mind's eye possessed drawstrings for the curtains of any room behind which human or animal coupling was taking place. With a lurch she had spilt into an anarchy of frenetic movement.

She'd got lost and found herself spinning out of control through a grotesque showcase of sexual give-and-take, down through the ages and back, finally wrestling herself to a halt with a giggling cook willingly leaning over a table in 1481 having her underskirts cut off with a blunt kitchen knife by a man dressed only in a brigandine and a sallet. Then, stuck fast as she was, it was in her struggle to escape from 1481 that she had realized she could slip beyond any scale of measurement. She turned one way, and found herself smaller than the size of smell in the woman's split end, beyond that point when mass is made up of any sensible particle, when it becomes a form of energy; twisting the other way she became so vast that light couldn't ever reach the end of her. For the first time she knew terror. She had to throw clamps on her lunatic knowledge.

How could she explain all this? She wound the platen on the old machine and looked at what she'd already written. It didn't seem *big* enough. She pulled the page off the bar and looked at it again. No! She crumpled it up and threw it away.

She became furious. Surely she of all people should be allowed to have more time, more of it. She thumped the table, then looked at her open hand. "Here!" she commanded, as though it would arrive, this extra time that she would need. But it wasn't like cake, you couldn't measure it like that. It was a phenomenon requiring a leap of under-standing even to begin to see how *different* it was.

61

Then, as often happened on these occasions, she became frightened. Time was such a faceless companion. So even-tempered it was sinister. Time was omnipotent, it was omniscient, but it never said a word.

She realized her mouth was open and that she'd stopped.

TWELVE

SANTAY TILTED THE silvery pistol back and forth in his hands.

"I know which end of this thing I'd rather be," he said.

"It looksa so dangerous to me," exclaimed Gabriella, "whatever end, the whole thing goes bang both ways."

Santay pulled the trigger several times, examining how the revolver moved. The alignment of each chamber looked uncertain, sometimes they lined up with the barrel, sometimes not.

"I don' wanna say to Mrs. Gorse," warned Gabriella.

"I'll tell her," confirmed Santay, "I'll pretend I found it in my room."

"She'll know this is no true."

"Maybe. Doesn't matter. She'll still have to get rid of it, she'll have to call the police and have them take it away. What else was in the trunk?"

"Big dusty books about war in India."

"Bring it all down. I'll pretend it was in the bottom of the wardrobe."

He held the pistol to his head. "D'you remember that film?"

"Don'!" she smiled. "I'll kill you if you do that."

Santay handed it back to her. "Come on, four-thirty, I'll be late. Get me outside will you?"

She fitted the pistol back in its case and pointed at the wardrobe, lifting her eyebrows.

"Yes, shove it in," said Santay, "it won't be there for long."

Gabriella hid the wooden box among his board games in the drawer beneath the wardrobe.

SANTAY PULLED ON the gloves that were scarred, worn in a line across each palm by the wheels of his chair, the gloves that were for proper runs, and thought, "This is how it should be." One girl—a friend—had asked his advice, but he hadn't been able to help much because he was off to see some other girl—another friend—who had rung up especially and asked to see him. A full life! Gabriella would help him with the steps so he didn't even need Molly. Perfect.

Pleasure lifted him as he gained the outside. At the bottom of the steps he swiveled and aimed for Victoria Station. Julia.

Julia had rung because she wanted to stop the worries that cruised up and down in her overcrowded mind without interruption, and he could do that for her. She wanted to walk around her preoccupations, explain them to him (she looked forward to the time when she could file them away).

She was walking across the station concourse with a new twitchiness in her paddling motion, Santay noticed. Her greeting was nervy, and she squealed with annoyance at the crowd as she wheeled him to the hot chocolate booth. He longed for the kiss on the corner of his mouth.

She landed in a bolted-down plastic chair; he parked himself next to her.

Santay's more ambitious longing: to free the buttons of her coat, then her blouse; inhale the first breath of her warmth; open up the underclothes and move in; to turn then and refasten the clothes from the inside, to squirm gently in her cleavage, maneuver himself between her breasts until he was facing outward with his ears growing hot and filled with the drumbeat of her heart, while her nipples—fiercely, proudly, one each side—watched out for him; to close his eyes and belong . . .

"How are you?"

"Don't. Don't ask." She shook her head.

"I'll guess. Are you going back to him? You must be taking the train?"

"No."

"Why are we here then?"

"What else is Victoria famous for?"

Santay couldn't think of an answer but it didn't worry him. He liked her riddles. He stirred his chocolate and floated the cup over his shocking thighs toward his mouth.

Julia leaked a giggle through a mouthful of chocolate.

"What?"

"Your bottom lip goes out like a dray horse's . . ."

Later he asked her what she thought she wanted from the immediate future. She answered with her customary earnestness.

"I only want two things. Not many, after all! Love, and money."

"You can have subdivisions," said Santay.

"Oh yes, love can be passion or affection or respect or sex, it can be something you build, or an accident you throw yourself into . . ." Julia rattled off such sayings.

"Money can be lots of money or enough money," Santay added.

"You know there's that saying from somewhere, about the future being a room that you can prepare before going into. The room needs decorating, furnishing, and an atmosphere just so, then you can go in. But it's not like that. I've been deceived. There are two or three rooms, and you can't be in them

65

all at the same time. You can't have everything at once, how-ever hard you try. It's like a stupid executive toy. In my case there never was a room anyway, it was a *trompe l'oeil*."

"You painted it yourself."

"Exactly," she exclaimed, "designed the whole thing. But then what d'you do when you discover it's not like that? Money there, love over here, sex somewhere else altogether—it's impossible. No wonder I started inventing. Now look where I am."

"Where are you?"

"I'm in a bed-and-breakfast. Victoria is famous for them don't you know."

"What happened to your friend's place?"

"Don't. I couldn't. Don't."

"So you're in a B-and-B?"

"Yes. Symbolism rubs it in sometimes, doesn't it?"

"I am *sorry* . . ."

"The worst of it is, I'm sorry for myself. No love. Not much money left . . ."

"Listen." Santay took her hand. She did not withdraw it. "You do have some of both of those. If you haven't, I have."

He held on for a while longer, then as if by agreement they wrapped their hands around the cups and talked, willing events to grow and happen. The booming station concourse protected them. People teemed, so they were hidden. Intimate question-and-answer sessions came quietly, lost in the huge noise.

Even after she'd left, Santay stayed in the station. The vast concrete arena was ideal: he could wheel himself freely among the crowds of people, and watch the business of others. His continuous searching for pretty faces, pretty bodies, drew him into sweeping perambulations, among strangers who streamed in any number of different direc-tions, a turbulent, worried human mass, all craving a desti-nation, or a departure.

66

THIRTEEN

THEIR HEADS TURNED in unison to catch the signal. There was a powerful torch bulb dangling from twin wires slung over the top of the wardrobe; it had lit up for a second or two, no more. They looked at each other and smiled. Gabriella lifted a finger to her lips to order silence; Marek dropped his hands. (Skim wasn't there to witness the first use of his landlady alarm.)

Mrs. Gorse continued climbing the stairs and stood swaying in the hallway. In her tight black dress she merged easily with the other trussed bundles; only movements marked her out.

She opened a bag of what turned out to be old clothes, which she then dumped on the floor. She leaned over, supporting her forearms with her thighs. At some stage in the past it had been sorted out, this bag, and she was trying to think where it should go: to Oxfam, or to the market stall of her friend in the East End, to be thrown away, or for the wash?

"Like an insect," Mrs. Gorse judged herself, "a giant species of hoarding insect."

Gabriella moved toward the door, but she stopped dead

when she thought she heard movement outside. Balance became precarious; her brows lifted.

Mrs. Gorse off-loaded one of her arms and burrowed into the assortment of clothes. Then rested again.

Gabriella waited, listening. There was no noise after all. She waved goodbye to Marek, and stepped quietly out of the door into the hallway.

Mrs. Gorse hoisted herself and clocked Gabriella coming out. The latter had sneaked from the room with wisps of hair escaping from the tie at the back of her neck, and her shirt tail was loose. Her voluble expression immediately collapsed when she saw Mrs. Gorse, who read the guilt falling across her face as hard evidence, whereas in fact it was proof only that the landlady herself was suspicious: Gabriella was guilty because the landlady expected her to be guilty.

Mrs. Gorse readied herself to make an accusation. She anchored herself on the terrain; this involved a straddling and a hand on the wall, like a field gun being secured before firing. Annoyingly, however, she was so flummoxed by Gabriella's sudden unearthly luminosity in the low-level, used-up daylight of the hallway that she failed to go off. She returned angrily to what she'd been doing before. Then she looked up again, and stood, silent, staring enviously. She thought, "Boys all around, like dopey flies moving in circles toward a pot of jam." And she had given permission for Gabriella's "boy" to visit! She pictured him: some Italian lout, some mama's boy with aftershave.

Mrs. Gorse recovered her tongue and gave Gabriella a smart whipping with her words.

"This is nonsense! It's stupid to chase all these boys! How old are you? It's the atmosphere of this house which is important to me. I won't have a *stupid* atmosphere! You have your boy coming. I let you have that. You can't have Skim and Marek as well. Moderate yourself! Watch out! Someone will *sew you up*!"

Gabriella stood, sullen, used to it, keeping a private distance between herself and the words of her tormentor. She cringed at the thought of Marek listening to the onslaught in his room.

Mrs. Gorse plucked the bag from the floor, pushed past Gabriella, and headed down to the basement, treading the way down one step at a time, thumping each stair heavily. Gabriella followed, watching her employer's feet. Perhaps it was only the trickery of her imagination, but she thought Mrs. Gorse purposefully stamped on Skim's switch.

Mrs. Gorse disappeared into her kitchen, while Gabriella continued down the corridor toward her box-room. She stopped by the toilet to see if there was any eavesdropping to be done (Mrs. Gorse often talked loudly on the phone, or to the cat). She rested her forehead against the doorjamb and whispered to herself, trying to control the inexplicable lifting of hysteria.

Complications gathered in her head. Sex as usual . . .

Warring judgments crowded her; there was that nasty background hum of Latin words that as a girl she had elided together to tie into a string of nonsense; ethics pressed on all sides; sinfulness glimmered attractively as the ridiculous equation struggled for balance: all bad pleasures on one side, endless repetition of certain prayers on the other. Presiding over the whole show there were the floating faces of her parents.

She didn't want her Catholic upbringing, but she didn't know how to excise it, except with sex. She wished for a simple taking-out of that part of her head. How much of her head would be left?

Yes, sex would end all this, but who with? Marek? Skim? Or Bruno?

Later, prowling round Santay's chair, she said, "I don't want him."

"Why not?" asked Santay.

"Because, of course, Marek. I am thinking about Marek, you know, all the time."

"But Bruno will be here soon, won't he?"

"Yes. But he's no really my boyfriend. I just pretend he is. Even so he will watch me like I have a biscuit."

"Have you talked to him about Marek?"

"He thinks if he comes he will prevent Marek. Aaagh!"

"What?"

"I am stupid. Like a book: open, shut. And too kind. If only I can be nasty, he'd stay at home."

Gabriella looked troubled. The strong dashes of her eyebrows were knitted together like caterpillars in a collision. Her eyes traveled over Santay's room, as if some actual physical clue might be found by which all difficulties would resolve themselves and her life become benign to her.

"What are you going to do?" asked Santay.

"He can't come. If he comes . . . He can't come."

"Then you'll have to tell him."

"I don' know," said Gabriella. "I am pretending to everyone. I am not true. I am caught by my own lies."

BRUNO ARRIVED ON a Friday night. Everyone was expecting a nice young Italian male, but he turned out to be a truly terrifying carpenter from Brighton. Six-foot-two, no socks, bare feet in his boots, a carefully chosen T-shirt under his jacket. Tattoos slithered over his shoulders and arms. A cloven chest; banked muscle on each side. His rib-chassis showed up spectacularly. His jaw was as square as a box.

Gabriella hid him down in the cellar, squeezing him into an uncomfortable L-shaped segment of the room.

They had a miserable evening. Bruno sensed there was something wrong. He made his approach—after all, it was expected of him—but he knew it was going to fail. He took it no further than usual: the girl's limbs flailing (all four); a look of terror on her face as though he was not only a stranger to her but a monster that had suddenly dropped its disguise. The first genuine scream stopped him.

70

He had his new jeans, his holiday wage-packet, but he wasn't wanted. He sat there in his corner, trying to be good fun until the evening was over.

Gabriella woke the next morning to find him sitting up in his bed, shaving from a mug of hot water.

"I'm sorry, you have to go," she said.

"Why's that then? I've only just arrived! Look how comfortable I am. What would you like to do today? We can do anything." Bruno tucked the blanket more firmly round his waist and twirled his razor in the mug as though he was stirring a cup of tea. With his smiling face partly covered in foam he looked like a debriefed Father Christmas.

"I can no have you here. Because, just because."

"I'm sorry about that, I really am," said Bruno, brightening up. "What's the matter? We had a laugh in Brighton." He considered her politely, then suddenly added, "Just because I'm a big guy doesn't mean I haven't got feelings you know."

"Is . . . is a problem," said Gabriella.

"Ah . . ."

"I've a boyfriend. Marek."

"Oh yes?" asked Bruno, "Marek, eh? That's great. It's to be expected, when you're young, more than one boyfriend." His heart was in his mouth, and chewed up.

"Here in the house," added Gabriella.

"Lucky old house," said Bruno, wincing at the sarcasm in his tone.

"So you muss go, please. Marek will be angry. I make a mistake. Sorry."

"Angry? I don't mind angry. I'll have a bit of that for myself maybe."

Gabriella frowned down at him, pleading.

"I'm happy here," continued Bruno, breezily, fermenting in sexual jealousy.

"Oh . . . !" moaned Gabriella in annoyance.

"Look how settled I am," said Bruno, "I can't just *go*."

71

He continued shaving, defending himself. There was silence except for the paddling of his razor in the mug.

Gabriella thought it best to leave him to it. Without looking up from the ground she left the room. If she stayed away long enough he would get bored.

Bruno waited, alone. He thought about the week's holiday pay, unused, still in the envelope in his pocket. He recalled boasting to friends of his good luck.

He couldn't go out to buy food in case he didn't get let back in again. He stayed all day and all evening in the basement, growing increasingly restless with worry. Gabriella returned once, but she left straight away without saying a word.

Much later, when he was pretending to be asleep, he heard her creep in. He felt comforted by her being there.

The next day, Sunday, Bruno found himself alone—again. He got dressed and waited, cursing. Nothing. The savageness of his hunger humiliated him, so he wandered, indecisively. Where was she?

He found himself upstairs. The closed doors blanked him off. He didn't have a clue which room they'd be in, she and Marek.

He walked in first on Claude and Molly. Claude had his hand on the side of Molly's neck; he withdrew it hurriedly and farted with embarrassment and fear. There was such a rambunctious wavelength to this noise, as though his buttocks had flapped together; his corduroys might have ballooned, briefly.

"Hel-lo!" said Bruno, as though he was arriving to tea. "I'm looking for Marek."

"Next door along, just there," said Molly, shocked, taking a step backward, away from him.

Following her instruction he opened the next door along. He saw a pair of shoulders mapped against a window, leaning over, working at something—the shoulders turned.

"Ah," said Bruno, "Marek?"

"Yes."

Bruno made a quick track of the room. Two unmade beds. There was a sense of evil described by the curled impression left printed on the sheets.

"I'm Bruno."

"Ah, as in Bruno and Gabriella?"

"Yes."

"Pleased to meet you."

Bruno was amazed. He waited, wondering what he'd hear next from this man's lips, from the body which was standing there so sickeningly near, within range of his anger.

"Pleased to meet *you*," he added, holding out his hand. Oh no! He dreaded these oily phrases sliding out. Why couldn't he say what he wanted to say?

They waited, until Bruno plunged in. "I know about the affair," he said, sounding delighted. "Gabriella told me."

"What affair?"

Bruno felt a charge of fury. He turned it into something else.

"Ah, I see, the evasive approach," he said, humorously.

"There was no affair," said Marek, concerned, "it wasn't serious. Nothing happened. Skim was there as well."

Bruno felt run through with disbelief. He started giggling uncontrollably. "Who was there as well?" he managed. "Of course, you were all there, having fun, well done . . ."

"We were having fun but not anything, not like . . ." Marek's vocabulary was not very good in this area. "Skim fell asleep," he added.

An unidentifiable noise came from Bruno. Everything was mixing in him: his hunger, his jealousy, the laughing crinkle of the sheets on the bed, this man's confident, mild look—he launched himself, arms outstretched. Both hands landed on Marek's chest and he pushed hard.

Marek flew backward into the table, then the wall. A brief grunt.

A moment gathering his breath. He'd banged his head. The floor reeled.

When he looked up Bruno had gone.

GABRIELLA LOOKED AFTER Marek's head, herself suffering from embarrassment. It became a joke, her constant ministering to his poor skull. But she was pleased. Her mind had been made up for her. And Bruno had conveniently disappeared—it was as though she had lost him. She half-heartedly went round asking if anyone had seen him.

No. Gone. Thank God!

But there was a price to pay. She became the unfortunate recipient of one of the landlady's notes, forbidding her as an employee to have any visitors or to collude anymore with the tenants.

The house quietened. Everyone was separate for a while in their different rooms.

FOURTEEN

CLAUDE POKED HIS nose round the door, briefly.

"Did you?" he asked.

"What?"

He came in and shut the door behind him, approaching Santay noiselessly as though he intended to trap him in an invisible butterfly net.

"Did Mrs. Gorse do something about the revolver?" he asked.

"Oh yes. Yes."

"What happened?"

"I told her about it, and someone came and took it away."

"So the revolver is completely off the premises?" Claude chopped the air with his hand.

"Yes."

"Thank goodness. The danger was that it could have got into the wrong hands. You never know, you never can foretell exactly where such a thing will turn up."

"I agree."

"Who took it?"

"A man from Her Majesty's Secret Service, MI5, I think."

"MI5!? How come?"

"Mrs. Gorse knows him personally. Or so she said. No questions asked. He would slip it back to the authorities."

"MI5. Extraordinary. She knows some extraordinary people. What was he like?"

"It was funny. He wore a gray raincoat."

"I don't believe it."

"Really," confirmed Santay, rolling himself past the computer. The cursor was winking at him from the top-left corner of the screen—it occurred to him to wink back.

"I will sleep easier in my bed," proclaimed Claude.

FIFTEEN

MRS. GORSE LOWERED herself onto the couch in the corner of her kitchen with a slight loss of control, so she thumped, gently, like an elephant going down. The tight black dress prevented anything but a slight bounce. She pulled the cushion under her face and felt the embroidery drag at her cheek. She squeezed her eyes shut to try and avoid the clairsentience . . . She was also trying to ignore pain.

Hawkins looked blankly at the recumbent form of his mistress on the couch, and jumped down from his position on the sideboard. With the formal manner of an English butler (it had earned him his name, after all) he stalked across the kitchen to the door, which stood ajar. He positioned himself in front of the gap, seating himself neatly. Every now and again his tail switched from side to side as he stared dreamily into the darkness of the basement corridor.

Mrs. Gorse was out visiting the future. The part of herself that could move out from behind her stertorous breathing was infiltrating the Royal Albert Hall.

She was looking down on the rank-and-file army of seats.

Tiny figures moved below her, taking their places. The orchestra was warming up for play, already sounding like a difficult modern score.

After a while the lights dimmed, obscuring the massed audience but leaving the orchestra more dramatically lit. Mrs. Gorse descended quietly, bringing with her the quiet hush that preceded the now imminent arrival of the conductor.

There was a solid wall of applause to greet him when he entered. Looking down on his scurrying figure as he negotiated the steps onto the stage, Mrs. Gorse could see the bald spot on his head shining like a beacon under the stage lights. A fringe of long, dark hair bounced around the rear edges of his head as he walked. He mounted the podium, acknowledging the audience before turning to the orchestra. The applause died away sharply. Having lifted his baton to draw the musicians toward a start, he gave one command. The orchestra, every instrument together except percussion, drew on one note. F sharp. There were scores of different vibrations sustaining the same note; the conductor listened intently, slowly resting his hands toward his sides and dropping his chin onto his chest. Dressed in black, he looked like he was standing at the edge of a grave. The note was still carrying around the hall; the cheek muscles and nasal passages of the musicians in the horn section won breath and the bows moved back and forth across the strings with minute slowness.

The conductor, still standing slumped, trying to bury himself in the sound, raised the baton and deliberately marked the air once, bringing a single *boom* from the percussionist which stopped the note dead. Only the hollow thunder of the drumbeats was left to reverberate around the giant hall.

When the conductor's head lifted, Mrs. Gorse was close enough to look into his face.

The music continued. Mrs. Gorse stared, fascinated by

the fully adult determination behind Marek's middle-aged eyes. The skin was blistered. His breath smelled of layers of alcohol of varying staleness. It looked like nothing so much as a sore face, and a face suffering at this moment as more blood vessels were unleashed onto the surface of the skin. The baton waved effectually at the crashing sound.

After the concert had finished Marek took one brief bow and left. The audience, some shamelessly standing up, demanded in vain his return for an encore.

SIXTEEN

W INTER ADVANCED. THE house grew colder. Periods of
sluicing rain from the low-pressure weather systems were
followed in from the Atlantic by their high-pressure coun-
terparts, and then the fine clean air moved slowly, the cold
swirling in from the north and shrinking the blood from the
outposts of its circulation. Pedestrians hurried outside the
door, hurried not just because of the cold, or the rain, but
because they were in a hurry.

Behind its glorious cream façade, whether it was
drenched in the streaming wet or frozen in brilliant sunlight, the house could get cold enough to stop a bullet.
There were enough air pockets in the central heating system
to make it practically defunct. The water pump clicked and
thumped with annoyance in its basement cupboard.

Mrs. Gorse turned to the student. "What are you going
to do with your life?" she asked.

"I don't know, I mean, I'm not exactly sure yet. After
college . . ."

"Do you think," Mrs. Gorse asked, leaning across the
table on her knuckles, "that it is important to have a *purpose* in life?"

"Yes, very important."

"What purpose do you have?"

"Well, like I said, I'm not sure . . ."

"D'you know what a purpose is?"

"Yes, it's . . ."

"But you don't have one yet. How can you know?"

"No, but I know . . ."

"A purpose is what gives a *meaning* to your future. You understand me? You have your future ahead of you. Your future is like a cake, a piece of cake that's made especially for you. But you have to eat it, whether you like it or not. If you are hungry the cake is delicious. If you are not hungry the cake makes you sick and ill. Understand? A purpose in life gives you hunger, it gives you a reason to eat the cake."

"I agree . . ." said the student eagerly.

"D'you believe in miracles?"

"No. Definitely not."

"Well you ought to. You ought to have some romance in you. This—" Mrs. Gorse rapped her knuckles on the table "—what is it?"

"A table . . ." ventured the student, quizzical, unsure.

"Nonsense," said Mrs. Gorse sharply, "it's not a table, not primarily! It's a miracle, it's a *bloody miracle* first, then it's a table afterward, d'you understand?"

She added, "And people worry about water into wine. It's frightening, how small your minds are, you young people."

They started up the stairs on the way out to the van.

"Not that I can help much. It's up to you. Everyone is alone. If they don't find their purpose they are lost. Watch out. Lots of people will try and give you one. For their own ends, you understand, for their own purpose. But that doesn't count."

THE HOUSE HAD been reorganized. Such was Mrs. Gorse's tactical finesse that Gabriella, who had until recently been

81

in disgrace, was now given a reward for having been punished so thoroughly: the tiniest room in the attic of the house, the one with a little kitchenette attached.

Gabriella was enjoying this surfeit of sudden favor. Santay was happy to hear her knock and see her again put down her cleaning equipment for a chat. She was full of herself, delighted to be talking again. She looked refreshed, newly confident, older, suddenly a more certain person.

"I have made up my mind!" she said, as she threw herself against the pillows on his bed.

"What about?"

"You know my kink?" she asked, hauling a blanket over herself.

"Yes?"

"Is gone. Bruno cured me."

"How? What happened with him?" Santay asked. "All I heard was Mrs. Gorse got noisy, and then it suddenly got quiet again. Now it seems back to normal."

"He came to stay, like you know. There I am, me and this man. In that tiny room we are, all by ourselves. He was very big, as big as the house, you know, shoulders like a doorway and all his arms and legs like levers. At exactly the same time, I want him, and I was frighten' of him. *Because* I was frighten' of him. My kink. He tried to 'ave me, oh yes. But I fought him, bloody hell I fought him right off. He realize I was serious—I ask him to go away completely. But he did no go. So I went away. Still he did no go. Instead he went upstairs and pushed Marek against the wall—*slam!* It was such a stupid thing, I suddenly saw how stupid and young I am with my kink and my lies. So my kink has gone. Too stupid."

Gabriella had put herself in a bad mood under the blanket. The scowl on her face stayed set like a mask above the brown hill made by her hip.

"Don't frown," said Santay.

"Why not?"

"Each time you frown you wear in the line a little deeper. If you wear it in too much it stays put."

She pushed her eyebrows up to lift the frown. Santay laughed at the mad staring face that she made.

"But how are *you*?" she said suddenly.

"I'm OK."

"What has been happening?"

"Nothing much. It's got bloody cold."

"Why nothing much?"

"Too tired to go anywhere much. I'm not sleeping well."

"Where d'you go, these times when you go by yourself?"

"To see Julia. She's brilliant, looks me in the eye, everything."

Gabriella wondered if she looked him in the eye enough.

Santay gave a cough, a failed laugh. He wheeled himself over to the cork board above his desk and took down the photograph that was pinned to the bottom left-hand corner. He rolled back over to her, and her hand appeared from under the blanket to take it from him.

"Who's that?" she asked.

"Me."

"Here? It's outside the front door."

"Yes."

"That was your motorbike?"

"That was *the* motorbike."

The photograph had been taken in the pouring rain. The Royal Enfield was clear enough with its bulbous petrol tank and clip-on handlebars, but the figure standing astride it was wearing a silver-gray anorak and a helmet, its identity almost lost in the downpouring of gray rain. It looked like a wet ghost.

"Did you fall off?" she asked.

"The front brake seized," Santay tapped the photograph, "that exact front brake there, and I flipped down the road like I'd been shot out of a gun. Onto the curb and into a concrete post."

83

Gabriella was not saying anything. She watched, holding her lip in her teeth, while Santay felt again a hint of the absurd shock. He could suffer it anytime he wanted, at will.

"I only remember scatting down the road at an unbelievable speed, and wishing that I could just stop and stand up. I don't remember hitting, or anything else. But here, in this photograph, I wasn't frightened of motorbikes. Now I am. When I see someone riding, I mentally point at them and ask, 'How do you dare do that?' "

"Is horrible . . ." said Gabriella, curling herself tighter.

"What I'm saying is that there must be a reason you're frightened of men."

Gabriella looked at Santay for a while, and then she said, "You don' like to talk about yourself, do you?"

"Not much," he replied.

"Why?"

"It's not very interesting."

"Maybe you mean you can no bear it that people might not be very, very, very interested."

"I suppose so."

"I'm interested," she said.

"So am I really," Santay said to her sad face. "I am absolutely bloody fascinated with myself."

Gabriella laughed at his luxurious selfishness.

Her thick, dark hair and the brown of the blanket and her skin such a deep white—she'd be better than Molly, but he couldn't use her. He liked to think of himself as a treat for her on her working round. Neediness would turn him into a dragging social weight, a duty, a chore.

He looked around the room: at the bar hanging above the bed, at the computer, its cursor blinking in the corner, at the little electric kitchen setup and the mini-bathroom in the cupboard.

He rested his hands on his lap, and watched his fingers as

84

he commanded himself to relax. They settled perceptibly, like he was dying. He felt his shoulders also sinking fractionally. They were both still.

Waiting, thought Santay. He suspected that many people were in the same state: going along all right, but essentially just hanging in the balance.

WITH DIFFICULTY, ACCOMPANIED by Marek, they got out of the house and in among the pedestrians who were fleeing past the bottom of the steps. It was as though the front door magically opened out onto a separate reality which moved at a frantic running pace through a different timescale, where the future seemed almost within reach, almost attainable, if only things could be hurried, if only there was just one more notch on the throttle.

Marek and Gabriella and Santay progressed at the slow pace of the world inside the house.

"Where are we going?" asked Marek, his voice muffled by the scarf.

"I don't know. Round and about."

They wandered along the pavements, interrupted by the curbs and delayed by road-crossing maneuvers. The cars skated along, diving onto their front springs or rearing up to take off again, the starting and stopping controlled (only just) by the changing lights. Among the proper people these three crawled along like a strange articulated insect.

They didn't talk much; they were preoccupied with personal thoughts.

As he walked, Marek tried to reach important decisions. The music wasn't going well; his piano teacher had accused him of wasting college resources. Should he go home or stay? He owed many people small amounts of money, and no sooner had he paid them off than he had to borrow it again. What kept him here, however, were the most important things: the music, the girl in the delicatessen, the sense

of growth and adventure and a breadth of possibility to life
. . . He had to stay. So what if he was poor? These last few
pence would do for a pot of coffee even if it made him sick
and giddy because the caffeine would work undiluted on
his empty stomach.

He thought about Skim. Why were they friends? There
was something Skim had—Marek couldn't put his finger
on it precisely—something like an idea, an experience of
somewhere that he himself had never been.

Normally he only became close to women, not because
he disliked men, but men wanted a friendship to race along,
they competed to exaggerate how brilliantly time could
pass between two people, or they just chased laughs. They
didn't want to go into it, or stay with it. Skim was an
unlikely male to be breaking the mold. He had been so
unfriendly to begin with. His sense of humor had been only
for his own use. He was cynical. It was as though . . . yes . . .
as though he were permanently *hurt* about something.
Marek felt a prickle of sentiment in his eye.

Where was it, this place that Skim was, where he himself
had never been? Marek watched the gas of his breath as
he silently enunciated the words, "Somewhere I've never
been . . ." The words were mysterious, encased in the
vapor, traveling out from his mouth, but silent.

They might get a free cappuccino if Ramona's boss
wasn't there. Some of these English words were strange to
him. Boss . . . boss . . . it sounded like a joke blow on
someone's head.

When they were sitting in the grounds of St. Peter's
church (recently destroyed by fire) Marek pulled the scarf
down from in front of his mouth and told them about his
home and how he loved it from a distance.

Afterward he leaned back in his seat and laughed and
shook his head. His hair, grown longer, furled over the edge
of the scarf and made the movement of his head look
dissociated from his body, like an owl's. His moustache had

a plaintive droop at each end of it now and he fiddled with these longer hairs, twirling them in his fingers to try and make them stand up on end. He looked content to be just sitting there, despite the evidence, the blood drawn away from under his skin, showing that he was cold. He glanced at the trees, and at the boarded-up ruin of the church, which looked particularly sad, being damaged. The magnificent status of it had been torn, dismantled. Anyone could see the secrets of the timber and stone—they were the same materials as used by any other building. It had been humbled; it languished. An imposing notice-board gave the figure needed to repair the building. The board itself looked in need of urgent structural work.

"We'll have another party one night," said Marek.

"Yes!" agreed Gabriella.

It was mercifully comfortable to sit with Marek. His personality exerted no pressure, there was no worry associated with his near presence. He was complete and self-contained, and since anyone while they were with him could borrow this for themselves, the feeling of loss when he went was always substantial.

He said, "I wonder how the church got burnt down."

"Probably struck by lightning for not being used anymore," said Santay.

"Why don't they mend it?"

"They're raising the money. Are you religious?"

"No. My parents are. I'm not. I don't see religion. But I have something, I think."

"What?" Gabriella was listening intently.

"A sort of faith, but in nothing. Nothing especially. Maybe that makes it in everything."

"Nothing but everything. Is brilliant," said Gabriella. "That's how it should be done. Is relaxed. Truthful."

She added, "Yes, it is the truthfulness that counts. It must be . . . Does it really matter if I am a virgin, d'you think?" she asked.

87

Marek looked up.

"What?"

"She's a virgin," said Santay, "she's wondering if it matters or not."

Marek's eyebrows rose in surprise. He hadn't expected that word.

SEVENTEEN

❧

Skim was moving the grandmother clock because he'd recently noticed that every time he passed by, the pendulum stopped. It didn't happen to anyone else. He'd investigated, and found that the clock was nodding forward when he stepped in front of it and this was interrupting the pendulum's swing. There was obviously a loose or broken floorboard, and he was heavier than most people in the house.

It was a magnificent piece of furniture. The wood had an ancient luster, despite being dusty, deserted on the landing. The mechanism was beautifully simple. It intrigued him. Skim ran his hands down the sides, bent his knees, and carefully hugged the grandmother clock. Yes, it might be an affection. He lifted it, and shuffled sideways, letting it down again gently. Miraculously it started ticking. Out of its return affection for him, he was proud to think.

He saw that a section of the skirting board had come loose, so instead of pulling up the carpet he removed that and peered in. There was a mess of wire and dust and wood. He dug around with his fingers. It was worse than he

89

had thought: the joist had come away from its support. Too much to worry about. Perhaps the clock would work happily in its new position. He propped the skirting board up, pushing some errant wires behind it. Turning to the authoritative clock, he set the hands to the correct position on its face and moved to switch the light off.

In the course of wandering here and there—back and forth to the bathroom on the first floor, to and fro on his way in and out of the front door—he had often noticed the anarchic routes taken by the antique rubber-insulated wiring. On these regular journeys within the house the slipshod appearance of the wires (escaping from behind the skirting boards or squashed into the corners without any clips) seemed to have gotten louder and louder in their demands for his attention, so when the light switch fizzed under his finger it was a warning.

He went to find the fusebox.

MAREK HEARD ABOUT it when he was getting into bed with all his clothes on. He was shivering with cold. It was ridiculous that he should be threatened with fire.

Skim was sitting up to his shoulders in the middle of a pile of blankets, so his head appeared as if from the top of an ice-cream cone.

"Empty," he said.

"Christ," said Marek.

"There's only one fuse for the whole house. One sodding great thirty-amp fuse. All the wires running under here," Skim pointed at the floor, where the scattered deaths of abandoned clothes and the litter of paper paraphernalia waited, ready to help the fire get off to a good start, "here, in the walls, up the stairs, across the ceilings to the center light-fitting, back to the light switches, behind the skirting boards, running all over the house, are ready to blow. It's a network of firecrackers. This house is like an electric bomb."

"So one mistake or accident . . ." said Marek.

"Light the blue touch paper."

"Blimey," said Marek. He leaned out to the lamp which stood now suddenly ready to explode or melt at the corner of the table beneath the window. He took the cord switch in his hands: "I hope this works all right." He tilted the switch to the Off position, and then back, repeating the test several times. Skim's face flashed—a series of woodenly serious expressions.

Marek left the lamp extinguished (it was safer).

They brooded, the pair of them, sitting up in the dark, facing the same direction, like a pair of mascots mounting a precarious guard against any unseen escape of electricity, and not knowing what to look out for.

"We'll tell Mrs. Gorse," said Skim. "She'll have to do something."

"What if she doesn't," prompted Marek.

"She will," said Skim, "she'll have to. We'll call the Health Inspector or something."

Their words flew in the darkness.

"We have to do something," said Skim from his corner. "What can we do?"

"Can't pretend to be all right, can we? What about a fire escape?"

"Escape to where? How?"

"First, a smoke alarm. And a rope. I'll buy a rope. If we hang it out of Gabriella's window, we can either climb up to her bit of roof, or down to the yard."

"I don't think I could climb up a rope that far."

"Down into the yard then."

"Maybe . . ."

They were both wide awake. The darkness turned them into children, they'd spooked themselves and couldn't rest.

Even after half an hour had passed in silence they were turning the same thoughts.

Skim put a wall of flames outside the door. He heard his own hair burning, a high-pitched sizzling sound like persistent insects. He'd escape first, then go back in to rescue others. The press, photos . . .

Marek had himself running around in flames. He tried to beat them out with his hands, but then he saw his hands on fire as well. Would eyes melt? He'd keep running, so fast that he'd put the flames out. Then he ran out of breath, and slowed, and the flames wolfed back around him. He fell to the floor and started rolling about. He could see a line of flames dancing on his moustache.

"I can't sleep," said Marek eventually. "I am watching for fires."

"We ought to go somewhere else. We ought to be brave enough to be stupid."

"Where? It's too cold."

"The car."

"The car?"

They had a brief discussion: should they wake anyone else? This would mean shaking everyone else out of their sleep and telling them that although there wasn't a fire at the moment there might well be one later that night so they were all to pick up their beds and camp in the street. They decided to go alone.

They stepped out into a wall of coldness, but that step carried such a load of relief because with the determination for action they believed themselves to have saved their own lives. As they crossed the street the chill gripped them, focusing on the only two warm bodies out and about. They hurried to the car, each carrying a spoil of blankets, Skim fumbling with keys. They threaded their way through the sleeping queue of parked vehicles toward Skim's large American sedan. Marek lay across the front seat, Skim had the back, and, lying there, they imagined the whole house roaring with flames, and slept.

THE NEXT MORNING the house was standing, just like the day before.

"It's still there," said Marek, as he shuffled across the street, feeling sore and cold.

"If we hadn't gone out to the car a fire would have started."

"You know what that means," replied Marek. "We have saved everyone's life."

EIGHTEEN

❧

"SHOW ME, SHOW me," Mrs. Gorse said defiantly, leaning on the back of a chair.

Skim led the way to the broom cupboard outside her kitchen where the fusebox was located. The screw securing the cover had already been lost, so he just lifted it off.

"There," he said, pointing at the single thirty-amp fuse and turning to Mrs. Gorse, who was leaning against the doorframe, her chest heaving with effort.

"There? What?" she demanded. "What is wrong with that? I don't understand."

"There's only one fuse for the whole house," said Skim.

"One house one fuse," snapped Mrs. Gorse. "How many fuses should there be?" Her eyes blinked fiercely.

"There should be a separate fuse for each circuit in the house."

"There *is* only one circuit in the house. From here to there to there to there to that room and then back here."

She added, "It must be good. Simon mended the wiring. He was a lovely man. He lived here for years. I trust him."

"Was he an electrician?" asked Skim.

"No. Don't be flippant! He was far too intelligent for

that. I don't have stupid people in my house. He was an administrative officer. He was a very . . . a very gallant and honorable man. A saint. I love him; love him, you understand? Love him! No, maybe you cannot understand."

Skim waited. Mrs. Gorse stared at the fusebox. Her head was skipping with different notions, there were too many goings-on in there, too much too fast, and all of it old, even these words she added: "What does this mean? Don't tell me what it is, tell me what it means."

"It means that the whole house is the fuse," said Skim, "and if anything goes wrong it won't be the fuse that'll blow. The house will blow instead."

"Blow? You mean blow apart?"

"Catch fire," said Skim. "If there is any fault the house will catch fire."

Mrs. Gorse pushed off from the doorjamb, launching herself like a boat from the banks of a river. She wheeled and went back to her kitchen.

Skim followed at a respectful distance.

He waited in her kitchen doorway while she stared at the floor.

"Oh my dear," she said, wiping one eye with her wrist and the other with the heel of her hand. Then she turned and advanced on Skim, barged past him out into the corridor again, and returned to the broom cupboard.

"Off, off!" she said, and reached up to lift the switch. The house went dark.

NINETEEN

❦

The upstairs folk of the house looked up, surprised by the electrical eclipse. They stopped whatever they were doing as though the switch that had plunged them into darkness had also momentarily incapacitated them. Some of them could have been expecting a visit from another planet.

Mrs. Gorse's voice was heard moving from floor to floor through the blackness. "An electrician . . . we have to have one . . . I'm sorry." But there was no electrician in the house.

Ironically this dramatic shift to safety consciousness scared everyone. Molly deceived herself by flying into a prolonged fit of common sense: she was happy to take charge of the store of candles and paraffin heaters funded by Mrs. Gorse, and trotted from room to room checking requirements, but at night she dreamed bad dreams about her nightgown going up in smoke. She had two, and both were flammable, so she ended up sleeping naked to try and calm herself, disappointing Claude who liked a tight band of rucked polyester across her armpits.

So there was a collection of small flames scattered, seeded

as it were, in every room: paraffin heaters showed their magic circles of toothed fire, greedily stirring the air with fumes that smelled of old diesel engines; candles burned with singular humility; one or two superior bottled-gas heaters gave off solid squares of heat, their delicate rear compartments hiding the monstrous bomb cylinders. It was impossible not to imagine that when conditions were right a raging crop of flames would take root—springing from wood, plastic, foam, cloth, hair, skin, eyes—and tear blindly through the house, leaving only the barren bricks and people's teeth.

A collection of red plastic "turbo" containers added an unlikely splash of color to the yard (full ones on the right, empties on the left; in between: puddles, showing off a slick new rainbow gleam).

Silence. No machine music, no toy-engine shavers or hair dryers. The angry Hoover stood disconnected, wound up, uselessly complex. There was no hint even of the talkative radio in Mr. Lightfoot's room before he bought batteries.

Claude fell downstairs, unable to see the banister. A lone tack that had been grimly holding the stair carpet in place sprang loose and he was scuttled, sent down by a furl of worn Axminster. He was ashamed. His bruises thumped in a sullen, smaller repetition of their original concussions, keeping time with his heartbeat. It occurred to him to kick the stairs but they were bigger than him. He was undamaged, but now he tested for the existence of each step before committing his weight, warning himself to expect a void beneath his size-eight Hush Puppies even when he was sure he was safely on the landing. It didn't help that he imagined men from MI5 lurking in the shadows.

Molly, worrying about his fall, took it on herself to distribute small disc-like candles on upturned wastebins at strategic points on the landings and in the lavatories. She lady-of-the-lamped her way round the house each evening, then sleepwalked and talked like a reject doll through the night, rising early to puff out the candles through her chapped, dream-encrusted lips.

TUESDAY, ELEVEN A.M., a missive from Mrs. Gorse to all tenants:

> I AM SORRY AND DESPERATE FOR MY OLD HOUSE. IT WON'T BE FOR LONG BUT EVERYONE MUST GO. THE ELECTRICIAN DOES HIS WORK AND THEN EVERY-ONE CAN COME BACK AGAIN. SEE ME.

They would all have to turn weary minds toward a packing-up and a finding of somewhere to stay—it was going to be a slow but temporary retreat from the house under adverse conditions.

Someone joked that old Mr. Clary on the third floor hadn't noticed that the lights had gone off yet, but he was the first to leave.

Marek was helping this senior tenant to the door. "The only. Thing I can't. Find is my spare teeth," he said, swaying on his feet, bent double, his body permanently cramped in a right angle, as though about to charge the wall.

There was a long stopping point made there, no progress at all, and for no apparent reason.

His frail head looked too vulnerable; one light tap and it would shiver, cracks would map its brittle surface. He lifted this kind elderly skull up a notch, as far as it would go, but it wasn't enough, he needed to lift his eyes to contact Marek's. His gaze had a watery depth as though struggling through from the bottom of a pond.

"I might as well. Have lost my. Sight as well. Not much use anymore. All I can see. Is a series of shapes coming toward me. God knows how I manage." Marek smiled. A second or two later a faint chuckle made its way out from Mr. Clary. He didn't move his lips; the noise came mysteriously, it had been breathed out by a small shaking of his back ribs. They took another step or two. "Don't mind an old fool like me. I'll go quietly. I'll go quietly . . ."

His daughter, herself helped by a walking stick, returned to lead him.

TWENTY

꧁W꧂

"WAIT," CRIED GABRIELLA.

Skim stopped attacking the window. She leaned in front of Skim and removed an empty fruit bowl from on top of the little table, and then lifted the table itself out of his way. Skim took a half step closer to the window, and thumped the sash with the heel of his hand. It refused to budge.

"Paint," said Skim.

Gabriella was upset at Skim's rough behavior with the window.

He asked her, "Have you got a knife, an ordinary kitchen knife?"

"What for?"

"To stick into the side here. Ram it in, break the seal of the paint, run it up and down both sides. The paint is like glue. If we cut through, it'll open up."

Gabriella opened a drawer sharply. It jumped open, with the rattling cutlery gathered at the forward end. She handed Skim a knife, and then left the room. Skim noticed her touchiness, but carried on forcing the window. When he'd succeeded he climbed out onto the small leaded square of roof to prospect for escape routes. A mountainous roofscape, but there—yes, and there . . . some were available.

Later, when it was dark, Gabriella went downstairs and complained to Skim that her window was now always an inch open. She'd preferred it how it was before, permanently shut, rather than open. It was the wrong time of year for a breeze. Skim got out of bed, pulled on his trousers, and returned to her little attic kitchenette. Candles flickered in the draft. His head caught the lightshade when he went in, sending its shadow swinging across the ceiling. The room seemed flimsy, careering back and forth. The table had already been moved out of the way for him.

Gabriella spoke to Skim's back, noticing how the shoulder blades moved like two side plates under his T-shirt.

"How can you possibly think she won't notice?" Gabriella began.

"I don't care if she does," replied Skim.

"She'll tell you to take it down."

Skim repeated: "I don't care if she does."

"You couldn't possibly climb up a rope anyway, not this far."

"It's not difficult when you know how. And we can always climb down into the yard. I think it's worth doing anyway. We'll tie it here . . ." He climbed out of the window again. The night claimed him with a cold punishment. The pattern of chimney tops and tiled roofs cut out against the orange and mauve sky made him feel like he was on a theatrical set, but not one that he had built. It was constructed on an inconceivably grand scale, with two or three stars figuring as distant lights. His carelessness escalated. He hissed and felt the nerves in his spine run, like they'd been stroked by a ghost pianist. There it was . . . He'd made himself drunk with the immeasurable distance. Christ! Where, what, was up there? He took away the stars, plucked them out, in order to see beyond. He pawed his way through space in an overarm crawl, eager for the

101

farthest boundaries. There was *not one* ... He felt saturated in nothingness. A nose-tingling sense of grand mystery invaded him. That corny, sentimental, brute power ... He swore softly, "Fuck!" He hung on to the feeling, hung on until the very last reverberation of magnificence had gone.

He felt a crick coming in his neck and lowered his gaze in annoyance, the pain bringing him back down to earth. He sat and tried to retrieve the sensation for a few seconds, but it could never be done—he knew this in advance.

Back inside he felt himself relatively powerful in the tacked-together cupboard of a kitchenette. Everything in it was so tatty and destructible—the tin draining board, the cupboards, the hysterical candles, even Gabriella. He knew that with just the weight of his hand he could smash the shelves, pull down the clumsy haywire plumbing. If he leaned against it he might even, he suspected, be able to demolish the outside wall and watch it fall into the yard below.

Gabriella was defiant. She cared even for the little table. She was proud of having this kitchenette attached to her new room.

He felt her eyes watching him to see that he didn't damage anything. He was stirred by her resistance.

After Skim had gone Gabriella felt the cool gladness of being alone. She would go and look in the mirror, perhaps, yes, for a long time.

It was a smaller mirror than the one she'd had downstairs. That seemed fitting. The candle spat in her hand.

She was determined to change herself. The new room had provided an inspiration for her to make the effort. She no longer wanted to control what other people saw when they tried to know her; that part of her will was gone. She wanted to be known, to be discovered by herself and others. Before, when she had used the mirror downstairs, she had always tried to catch a glimpse of the person that

102

others saw; she would strike facial postures that she believed to be nearly spontaneous, which was impossible because a mirror never reflected a candid image, always a contrived one. Now she didn't try. She looked simply at the reflection. She recognized its limitations, she tried just to relax. She told herself to admit that she was doing it, to own up and not damn herself for her very ordinary vanity. "Honesty!" she commanded to her mirror. She stared into her own eyes. What was there, what was really there? A tiny replica of the flame in each one. Everything was reflected. She felt riven by a fearful sense of insecurity.

TWENTY-ONE

❧

IT STARTED TO snow. The outside of the house, with its two neat white hats, one on the roof and the other on the porch above the front steps, now looked like an outsize model of an expensively decorated cake.

Steering Santay's chair required a gloriously slight effort on the slushy pavements.

Santay demanded to know: "What *is* it?" Skim lifted the bag out of his reach.

"Ah, wait and see . . ."

Santay wondered: what treasure had the house given up? A volleyball net, maybe—it had to be, considering this trip to Hyde Park with a football, which occasionally escaped from Skim's arms, to the annoyance of others.

"It's a secret," said Marek.

Santay had a secret of his own . . . He imagined he might land up in prison. Should he give up the pistol? It was romantic to take it out of the box and examine the intriguing trademark inscriptions on its barrel. Maybe there would be a dire change in the political climate. He put himself and the gun in his room, trapped, storm troopers kicking at the door. He had himself loading rounds in the chamber, whispering thanks to himself that yes, he'd had the foresight to keep it all these years.

He had got as far as loading the pistol. The extra weight had hung noticeably on his wrist. With utmost care he'd brought his finger near the trigger guard, and then, summoning bravery, he'd rested his skin against the old-fashioned mechanism. An enormous responsibility had descended on him; he'd started shaking with the weight of life-and-death power in his hand. He'd recalled Gabriella's words: ". . . bang both ways." The secret was all his.

They nodded along, pressing ahead through the condensation of their own breath.

In the park they untied the bag, still not letting him see, then held things up at a distance.

"Guess!"

Two giant cups dangled in front of him.

"A contraption for making yogurt," he called.

"NO . . ."

"A harness for a horse."

"NO!"

He could see it was a bra, but even so, it was amazing.

They tied the garments together. Santay held one end of the line of underwear, while the other was tied to a tree. Skim and Marek played a low-level version of volleyball. The ball was batted back and forth, while they stumbled after, chasing to intercept and hook it back before it hit the ground. Their knees got sopping because they fell trying to dab at the uncontrollable football. No score was kept, but Skim liked feeding on the sensation of victory, so he played hard. Marek took it as more of a game, trying to keep each volley going for as long as possible. At a certain point he took the ball in his hands, clambered over the underwear, and was about to throw the ball to the ground when Skim rushed him and they collapsed into the snow. One of Marek's feet was caught— Santay felt a jerking on his hand. It occurred to him that he'd caught a large friendly trout on the end of a line.

It was an achievement, seeing these antique pants flagged out in the park. Each of them secretly acknowledged the curious attention of passersby, but the garments were so huge and misshapen it would have been difficult for anyone to have recognized what they were looking at. Santay more than the others felt proud and funny in front of the strolling people. Although they were just walking past, entrenched in overcoats, giving no more than curious glances, to him they might as well have been all silently and invisibly clapping.

The snow was still clean, an immaculate carpet that doubled the volume of light. They were reluctant to go back into the darkened house and have to shrug off its closing atmosphere, so on the return journey they progressed more slowly, stopping to charge themselves with the altered landscape of the park.

"What you need," said Marek, during a long delay centered on a park bench, "is a weather switch on your heart. Hot, Cold—and you flip it to Cold for increased heartbeat and blood pressure." Skim didn't answer, and Marek turned to see the Walkman in position. He levered himself to his feet, thumping his hands on his thighs in a monotonous four-four to throw the blood down to the end of his fingers. "Instead you just have to keep moving," he said.

He continued tapping on his legs.

Skim spoke far too loudly. "What is music? I mean just what the fuck *is* it?"

Marek peered at him from between his felt coat collars. "Don't you know, stupid?" he shouted back, tut-tutting and shaking his head. "It's that sound you get when you switch on the Walkman."

"I love Marek," thought Skim, quite suddenly. "I was a wreck before I met him." He'd done nothing, back then, but chase his own cynicism, quarreling with it, *fucking* all the hatred he'd had, spawning other little hateful hatreds, so spastic they could only turn in circles. Depthless, black ideas had become overworked by his intoxicating anger. That incongruous stalemate within himself! At times it had seemed as though it was going to get dangerous. He'd felt like a heavy sailboat turning about, the prow drifting slowly to point toward rocks. He might have been smashed to bits. Marek had steered him—his was the lightest possible touch of friendship. It was not as though he had done anything. There was no change of opinion, no new formula for life, no opinion or philosophy suddenly introduced into his system. There were perhaps just the simple things like this game in the park. Marek being there was valuable.

Still his mind circled and aimed at possibilities. He measured the distance between himself and vague, possible goals set in the future. They would disappear if he tried to get closer to them, but now he was relaxed, fatalistic. It would happen. He trusted it to happen.

They continued onward, heading for home.

Santay braked, stopped. The others turned. The Albert Memorial behind them made their smallness seem part of a splendid design.

"You go on," said Santay, "I'm going to roll round for a bit."

An uncertain look at each other, then they waved and turned away. An old lady in the middle of the path moved between them gratefully.

Santay wheeled and went back in the opposite direction. He had ages to wait. He turned right, picking up speed on the cleared path to give his lungs a blow. He pushed harder still on his wheel rims. He'd go for a spin all right. He wanted to be hung-dog tired, so exhausted he wouldn't be able to sit upright . . . He felt his breath arrive. He'd go as far as he could, burn up the time left until his rendezvous at the corner of Serpentine Lake.

He still had to wait. He sought tea in the café, and settled down for the remaining quarter of an hour. What would

Julia be like here, where he had never seen her? She might wing her way in over the water like a gull.

When she came they decided on a circuit of the lake. Julia walked, he rolled beside her. People were strewn along the path—they looked darker, cut more clearly, and more interesting than usual. All individual clouds had dissolved into an absolute white. Kids were burning energy inside their rich warm wrappings. The tea had dropped through his system like molten lead and was threatening to pierce his bladder.

"Still got the ring?" he enquired.

Her hand came out of her pocket, flashed, and returned. "What can I do with it?" she replied. "Where does it belong now? I can't sell it."

"Give it back?"

"Tried to."

Santay held his breath. The black water crept up in endlessly failing wavelets against the edge of the pond.

"Is it done?" he asked.

"Oh Gawwd," she said, "it's taking days. Days and days, saying the same things as I said before, but this time in bizarre public places—in parks, in cafés. I've lost so much sleep. I could crash out right there." She waved at the ground in front of her.

"I'm sorry, must be grim."

"It's bloody funny sometimes. We have laughed like maniacs. Like loosing the tap that holds it all in. But then it's serious, so deadly serious. Especially when we talk about money. And I have none left! Less than none, not even access to debt anymore. He seems to think this is simply the price I have to pay for independence. My new status as a bag lady approaches."

"You won't starve. My offer still stands. It's silly to repeat it, but you know . . ."

"Thank you. It means a lot. I need that offer to be there."

"It's there."

The trees stood frozen. There would be another tree beneath the surface, a tree of roots, like an invisible mirror image, except muddy and wildly unformed. The trees looked like they were waiting for him, Santay thought, ready to wait a long, long time. They had that studious optimism.

"I don't dare look at my future," continued Julia. "It's too empty. There really is *nothing*. Just me standing in an impenetrable squall of bad weather."

"That's a start," said Santay glibly, "then there's the clothes you stand in, and your handbag. Your looks. Quite a lot really."

"It feels like nothing. Or rather like nothing so much as a rush toward my grave. The lid's off my coffin. Men far below are standing round waiting for me to fall in." She shivered.

"Maybe they're standing waiting to catch you, to stop you from falling in."

"I wish they'd say something then."

"Hang on," said Santay, mocking up an urgent tone, "just waiting around are they?"

"Yes!" she exclaimed.

Santay was itching to wave, to make a claim, but he kept his hands on the wheels. "Oh I know that lot," he said; "yes, waiting to save you, they are."

"I look forward to meeting them," said Julia.

MRS. GORSE BEGAN speaking her sentence shortly before broaching Santay's door; he only just had time to bury the shamefully trashy women's magazine he was reading.

"No." She stood, heaving, square in the doorway. "I'm sorry, I can't leave anyone behind here. And I can't take anyone new even for a short time." She could say this easily and with unequivocal conviction because she was frightened. She was worried about deterioration. It seemed to be

109

eating away around her. It had an appetite. Her constant bitter pill, that nothing could be avoided or even altered in the slightest, allowed for virtually no hope.

"All these candles," she continued. "I don't want anyone to be burned alive in their beds." Burdened by the accumulation of *déjà vu*, she often looked as though she was trying to sharpen her eyes by blinking, even when she was saying something quite ordinary. "So I am emptying the house. Yes, everyone. Before Christmas. Then I have the wiring done. Then everyone can come back. Well, not everyone. Those that are good with their contributions, yes. So tell your friend she cannot come. I am sorry, but I am thinking of her, I don't want her to wake up dead, like a cinder in her bed. She will blame me. Tell her I'm sorry. After Christmas."

Mrs. Gorse rotated, using a sturdy rocking motion, and left.

TWENTY-TWO

MOLLY KNOCKED AT Santay's door. He knew it was her knuckle; it made a particular sound: timid, grateful that it had been allowed. He imagined it curled up in a cringing position and tapping.

Her terrible face appeared (following the dutiful wait for a reply) and she made her sensible offer of help.

"Do you feel," she said with leaden respect, "that you need a smoke alarm in here? There'll be one in the corridor, but you might want one in here as well."

She was going to use her own savings (she had been struggling for years), partly to put toward the cost of the rewiring and partly to pay for anyone who needed a smoke alarm and couldn't afford it. Santay said he wanted one with an emergency light in it.

A uniformed electrician could be seen every now and again poking about with a torch and measuring. He'd consulted with Mrs. Gorse and presented a work schedule on a piece of graph paper. Deadlines were set.

The exodus of tenants took place gradually; it was more of a dribble than a rush. There was very little fuss. Some tenants merely packed a suitcase and went to park themselves with

friends, leaving the main body of their possessions contain-
erized in tea chests and cardboard boxes, each of a weight
easily shifted by the electrician. Others were moving on to
some other place. A careful weeding-out of non-paying or
noisy guests took place. Numbed by the rise in rent announced in typewritten notes found on their pillows, they
left more quickly, blown along by bad moods, with their
bags bumping angrily behind them.

Claude and Molly moved out together, Claude anxiously
hiding all his stuff behind two armchairs in the hope that no
one would touch it, and Molly hobbling after him with
chilblains tacked to her toes. Even Mr. Lightfoot had gone,
his radio's creepy electric voice finally killed off.

Marek saw into their rooms as he climbed the stairs.
Every time he went up he noticed which new door was
standing open. The abandoned stance of the doorway
would reveal a more or less large slice of a private room.

Marek wound up past these landings more and more
often. Gabriella no longer had to clean the house, so they
had hours stretched out for them to be together. Often
they lay entwined like brother and sister. Neither had
much to do with these winter days. It was enough for each
to grow familiar with the smell that hung on the other's
heat, and the conjoining of their differently weighted
bodies.

Marek allowed her to groom the patch of flaky skin
between his eyebrows.

Gabriella's admission, she badgered him until he agreed:
she had an incongruously old neck for such a young
woman.

Marek was puzzled about his feeling for Gabriella. What
was it? He gave an answer on each step: an easing; a
delight; a louder sigh of satisfaction . . . There was no doubt
that this was happening, but why? Perhaps because there
was no one else? Ramona at the delicatessen had become
too repetitive, her vague dreams adding up to nothing, her

problems recurring, her small battles dragging out. If she had been a great musician this might have been forgivable. Gabriella had changed, he decided. As he climbed the last set of stairs she side-stepped into view above him, silently, like a ghost. He rose toward her, sounding the usual greetings. When he reached the top they were standing close; she became absolutely clear, even her expression was sharp in his focus.

He could see her properly, that's what had happened. He understood her now. She had come within his range.

Their knees scuffed together as they fitted themselves round the small table in the kitchenette. They talked about their plans. She wanted to be a teacher back in Italy. He didn't mind where he lived as long as he had a piano under his hands and time to use it. Perhaps he could teach a class in music, she suggested.

He thought that love, real love, should mark the start of adult life. She thought it would do that anyway, whether it ought to or not.

It was a favorite for them to work on, the subject of love.

"You can fall for someone in just a day, or an hour, I'm sure," said Marek.

"In one look," said Gabriella, "you can have passion just in one blink."

They stopped there, the point suspended, because they were both aware that whatever it was between them it was not the result of some such blink.

TWENTY-THREE

Six P.M. AFTER work—Julia needed help urgently. Her life had broken up completely, the wreckage a few boxes at her feet.

She turned up at Chapel Street for her run-in with Mrs. Gorse. Santay bumped down the stairs, she was the brake. With the two saucered candles lighting the way it was a ceremony. Santay knocked, and found the landlady sitting behind her typewriter, peering over her glasses.

"Yes?"

"Mrs. Gorse, I just wanted to introduce you to someone . . ."

Julia stepped forward, swaying from one foot to the other, her hands knotted in front of her midriff. She released one to hold out to Mrs. Gorse.

"This is Julia," said Santay.

Mrs. Gorse frowned at Julia's hand as though she'd never seen one before.

"What d'you want?" she asked Santay. "Can't you see I'm busy?" Julia withdrew her hand and threw an emergency look to Santay.

Mrs. Gorse had cottoned on—she was remembering her

earlier refusals—but he knew a way round the back of her. He'd have to play on the urgency of the situation.

"Julia's got nowhere to go," he said. "She has to come and stay with us."

"Has to, why has to?"

"Perhaps I ought to say," began Julia, firmly. "My marriage has broken up. I've got nowhere to go. Can I stay for a week or two while I find my feet?"

Santay enjoyed surfing on the immense pride that rose in him—she'd picked up on his tone and used it herself.

"Your marriage is it? You're the girl with the marriage?"

"Yes."

"You gave up?" queried Mrs. Gorse.

"No," said Julia emphatically. "I made a mistake."

"Oh dear! What was that? What mistake?"

"I imagined for too long that I was somebody else."

"Somebody else? How can you be somebody else?"

"I tried to make myself suitable for someone else."

"Nothing wrong with that. That's no mistake when it's your husband. You shouldn't give up on that, you should be trying even harder young lady."

"Not when I'm damaging years of my life, and years of his. I can't get them back or have them again."

"No, indeed not."

"I had to think of him too. It's like living in a corrupt state. Because he didn't know."

"Corrupt. But you were the one who was corrupt. Mostly corrupt just by yourself."

"Of course. Almost entirely by myself. He was sincere. But if it's rotten for everybody there's no point in trying to be good about it."

"What did he say to this split-up?"

"He agreed eventually."

"Sounds like a torture scene, 'He agreed eventually.' Does he love you?"

"He did."

"So you betray love by moving out?"

"No! I betray love by staying with him. His and mine."

"Oh my Christ, yes, that's awful. No you mustn't do that. To betray love is like eating with your mouth open. Grotesque. And bad manners. Because love is a gift, you know, an absolute gift. What sort of man is he? Weak?"

"No. But not strong."

"Is he alone now?"

"Yes."

"And you, are you alone now?"

"Completely."

"Oh my dear," said Mrs. Gorse; a look of pain was arriving on her face, Santay was glad to see. "Where are your things?" she continued.

Santay answered for her. "There's only a few boxes. I thought we could put her in Claude's room."

Mrs. Gorse began to speak to Julia in her wartime voice: "Yes, yes, your dignity, whoever you are, you must have your dignity like another box, like a Christmas present from us. Now! Do you understand, that is who I am inviting to stay, not you, but your dignity. Go—go—go, Santay will show you your room."

Santay reversed, suppressing elation. Julia followed. As their eyes met, private again in the stairwell outside Mrs. Gorse's door, he raised his fist in a candle-lit salute. "Yes!" he muttered, smiling past clenched teeth. Julia fluffed his graying hair.

Later, standing alone in the unfamiliar room, Julia felt ominously free. She had launched herself; the horizons that she had avoided, that she had purposefully kept at a far distance, were now coming up and disappearing underneath her like in a video game. She was so loose her limbs might unhinge and fall.

"And sex everywhere," she thought. In her streets people would be taking their clothes off and yanking at each other. Grunts only. On her tube journeys people's buttons would

116

be pinging, their ties ignored in the furious chase to the chest, to the insides of their pants. She'd be out running with no shoes on, chased by men, falling to the ground and pretending to try and escape while she got done.

In this respect breaking the bag-lady barrier was clean good fun. The fall had been exhilarating. She wondered how long it would take before she started trying to build her way out of it.

She toured her borrowed room. "Home," she thought. It occurred to her to turf out the stuff piled up in the corner. The bed was made up. She noticed a small triangular tear in the pillow slip, the flap of cotton starchily threatening her. There was the smell of stale incense. Someone else's possessions though—annoying, that. Her own boxes were huddled by the door like wet puppies.

She paddled back and forth as she arranged things in the first-floor room.

Skim was on his way to the bathroom the next morning when he glimpsed Julia's hair, standing out with static, floating past in the doorway. He was strongly inquisitive.

When he went in she was making the blank iron bed, dressing it as a throne, or altar of luxury.

"Good morning," he said.

"Hello."

"You must be Julia. Are you all right?"

"A bit unnerved. Browbeaten. A bit of a drowned beetle."

"Some beetles can swim."

"Well this one can't swim very well," replied Julia. She turned her back, busy.

"I'm Skim."

"Hello. Julia."

Skim realized he was being rude, standing uninvited.

"Sorry, I was surprised to see someone there."

117

"That's OK."

He relaxed. After all, she'd be around.

FIVE-FORTY-THREE P.M. SKIM returned to his room and toyed fretfully with a few tools on the table.

Was she up there?

He felt like getting busy over something. What? Marek had made the little clay candle holders ... He dipped his hands in the little bucket of cloudy water and scooped a double handful of clay from the bag by the side of the table, mulching it in his hands. He'd try something different. He felt a school of nerves shiver over his back.

HAWKINS SAT ON the table in the basement kitchen, examining Mrs. Gorse's face with a professional manner.

Mrs. Gorse was poised over a blue square of paper. She had never felt so alone.

She felt Skim's thumbs tearing at her sides (there was the burning sensation). It was a repeated motion, her flesh was being dragged off. The hands changed position to clamp round her head or her torso. His thumbs drilled into her eye sockets, digging halfway into her head. When fingers pressed into her neck she felt panic: the breath was being stopped in her body.

Hawkins weaved his nose forward small fractions; his look narrowed.

She took the pounding on her shoulders and the tickling as Skim sprinkled tea leaves on her head. "Tea leaves," she managed, "I ask you!" Her hair was thin and cut quite close to the skull, but she didn't agree that it looked like tea leaves.

She glanced down to see, as if from a great distance, her hand moving across the paper. It was a letter to a friend. The scrawled inkwork would finish soon. She cursed Skim.

To be made up as a dummy, a Plasticine grotesque! She rose to her feet.

She stamped on the third stair as she went up. She hated it. Skim's switch. She felt her eyes pop and burn as though a photographer's flash had gone off in her skull. For the first time she was *pulled* then, dragged off. Someone of her skill! To be kidnapped by that clumsy oaf. To watch his thoughts passing like vessels overloaded. The slops of his mind crawling with junks. Firework phrases about youth went off in her head. "Bloody young! So new, so shiny new! Nothing in their brains. Empty as coconuts." She frowned. "Just a few vanities, some milky ideas. All experience is lost, wisdom is thrown away on youth!" She was appalled. "Only knowledge, knowledge dangerously written down, is left," she muttered.

The treadmill of the stairs continued. She trod and trod, rising like a mountaineer, blind to the present moment.

She saw a hundred thousand of Skim multiplying away from her on all sides, a gallery of four-dimensional mirrors reflecting different times for him.

Some beckoned—a loud voice calling from a stage. She saw she was among a small gathering of students waiting to learn about stage management. Skim (he had a moustache!) ignored the agenda. He stood facing the audience and spoke freely, with conviction. He was demanding that they ask themselves something. "What is music?" he was saying. There was a silence, the students were puzzled and embarrassed. Two lads whispered. One made a clicking gesture with his hand—it looked like he was trying to throw his fingers away.

"What is light?" Skim continued, careless about the giggle from the back row. "What is life itself? What is it"—here he paused for emphasis, and gave time to considering a few individual faces as though it was something he had recently picked up in a public-speaking manual "—what is it that makes the difference between being an animal and a human being? I'll tell you. It's an awareness, an awareness of . . ."

Mrs. Gorse found herself borne off by a disturbed shuffling of feet and a sudden hum of disbelief. This lecture was meant to be about stage management. The students were ashamed of him.

She continued to struggle for an escape. She used the usual devices: trying to see her feet, seeking the comfort of her physical weight, listening for Hawkins. Unsuccessful, she floated through a workshop where Skim was repairing clocks. A pair of magnifying lenses rested on his forehead. He was moving a lamp, clumsily, aiming it at some problem. Hawkins's eyes flashed in the gloom as the light flitted past his usual place on the horse blanket.

She saw her own black shoes still rising like machines to reach each stair. It was difficult. She was worried about the return of her breath. She felt a gain in weight, but it was as though she was pedaling her feet in a vacuum.

On an equal level with her face, on the topmost landing before Gabriella's attic, Hawkins waited to meet her gaze. He was seated, his tail scything evenly from side to side.

"Hawkins," she cried, her *déjà vu* settling a layer at a time as she accustomed herself to her return, taking up the unavoidable thread of her life's run. "Where have you been? I have been looking. I don't want to lose you. Now listen. Be grown-up. Don't be adolescent!"

She took the cat up onto the shelf of her breast. He put up with it, looking down as though nothing so undignified was happening. She ran a jumpy hand down his back.

TWENTY-FOUR

There was often this gathering in Skim and Marek's room to share the best bottled-gas heater. Comments were passed over the top of the storm lamps. Nothing was said that was of much importance.

Skim lay in bed, eating sugar products. It would have suited him better, as a bulk consumer, if they didn't bother to spend all this money on inedible packaging. His practiced fingers broke through the fancy designs mercilessly. He was an expert. At that moment he was going through a phase of eating boxes of party meringues.

Marek shared his corner with Gabriella.

How closely set were the boundaries of their appreciation of time. In that room they were time-blind. The future was a limitless space, and for their use. A share of seventy-odd years seemed impossible to use up. To look so far ahead was like trying to comprehend the distance of a star—they knew they'd get lost if they tried. Nevertheless each one of them had a manifesto for what was going to happen to them beyond the next three weeks.

When Julia appeared with Santay there was a friendly

silence. Santay parked himself, reversing like a car into the slot beside the big chunk of wardrobe.

"God," said Julia, picking her way among wine bottles and other debris, finding a corner for herself and pointing quickly at several things (the candles, the storm lamps, the clay figure on top of the wardrobe, Skim in his bed with an arm behind his head, the elbow hoisted toward the ceiling as though in a defiant gesture), "it's like Dickens."

"*Wuthering Heights*, eh?" replied Skim.

Nobody said anything.

Julia and Santay were aware that even slow moments like these remorselessly accumulated to lay, eventually, such a weight of moments on them that would see them into their graves. The others were like cartoon figures who had strolled off the edge of the cliff and were now miraculously walking in a void, able to do so only because they hadn't yet looked down.

Skim was already in love with Julia. It was a predictable response to her interesting beauty. So he hardly spoke. The others continued by themselves, leaving him madly staring out from his corner. What was said was ordinary: they were preoccupied with having to move out, with the nearness of Christmas.

Later, when the condensation on the windows had grown to an impenetrable opacity and the conversation had tired to just the odd restful comment, Santay decided to roll himself back to bed.

"Drunk in charge of a chair," he said. Everyone got up; Skim opened the door. Julia made her way to Santay's side—she would have been embarrassed to have been left in the room.

Skim patrolled for Julia outside the door, assuming control of Santay's chair so they could both go down together. When they'd reached the half-landing Skim relinquished his grip and said goodbye in a curiously hard voice. Julia ducked to kiss Santay on the cheek, bumping her nose against his: it was dark.

As he shut the door on them Santay felt uneasy. They were both there, standing like blackened posts, facing into his room. Had they wanted to come in, for some reason? He sat for some time, reluctant to spoil the sociable warmth of the alcohol. The ignominious effort of getting himself unclothed and in the bed could be put off. He hardly slept much anyway—in fact he felt more wide awake at night than he did during the day. He considered, with the blanket under his fingers feeling like the skin of a teddy bear, whether or not he should haul all the bedclothes onto him and crash out in his chair, but he had been taught a score of times (by a sore neck) that he would regret it. The bar hung above his bed, ready. He waited, enjoying the thump of the drink in his head.

Then the evidence came, as a sound, and as a vibration through the brickwork: the click and low shudder of the front door closing.

He drew a cigarette very slowly from the packet. He stared at it. He didn't own Julia—he was quick to remind himself of that. But it was cruel . . . He had a drunken thought that he would never, ever hold her in his hand as certainly as this cigarette. With pretend ceremony he pegged it lovingly between his lips.

SKIM HAD ASKED Julia if she wanted to go out for a walk. She'd not been surprised at the quick offer thrown by Skim just as she'd turned upstairs toward her own room, but she'd been startled by her easy acceptance; she was shot through with thrill. An idea occurred to her, it was as strong as a voice actually whispering it in her ear: if she couldn't find this perfect room that represented her future, or if she couldn't make the room happen, as she had tried to, then perhaps she could have two or three rooms, and visit each one in turn.

It was, relative to the past weeks, quite mild, and the air was saturated. They walked for a while, then ducked into a little square, a patch of green spiked with dog mess and surrounded by a fence with a hole in it. They sat on a bench and looked around themselves, fumbling against social discomfort.

There was only one window that showed through the trees: a square of light. They made guesses as to what was going on in the room behind the light. They thought there might be a seduction.

After more guesses they ran out of that idea for talking.

She noticed the effect of his weight on the bench: when he leaned back the whole big solid thing moved as if it was a flimsy fold-up garden chair. She'd never met anyone with such careless physical strength.

Talking seemed very necessary. Skim asked, "How did you meet Santay?"

"At Victoria Station. We were both handling coffee and doughnuts. He said, 'Snap,' and we got talking. We've had some times in that place."

"What sort of thing?"

"Nothing much. Looking at people, making snap judgments, you know, inventing people as they walk past."

"Yes!"

"Tell me a story," she said.

He was put off by this demand. He felt stupid. He didn't know what to do.

"I'll tell you one then," she said, starting easily as though she'd had it prepared. "There was once a beetle living at the bottom of a bench leg," (she pointed) "and it was in a bit of a state, so it couldn't exactly . . ."

Julia stopped. Skim's hand was shifting the fabric of her dress into a pile on her lap. Her knees appeared, looking absurdly decorative topped by so much flowered print.

124

Skim knelt in front of her, a hand on each of her knees. He lowered his head and took a pinch of flesh between his teeth.

Julia leapt to her feet and ran, hopping over the ground but then cracking her head as she went through the gap in the fence, which made her furious.

Skim pursued her. His entreaties were met with silence. "What's up ... I'm sorry ... Look ..."

They continued homeward with Skim trailing a few paces behind, bombarding her with questions to start with, but then giving up because she refused to answer.

When he turned the key and stood back she went in without a word. He watched her disappear up the stairs and then he walked slowly up himself and stood in the now empty space where the waving shadow of her skirt had last been in sight. He looked at the handle of her closed door, waiting for it to turn.

He was excited—he sat on the top stair and marveled at how he felt. The cartoons were accurate. Eyes really did fall out of their sockets, that's how it was. Not the touch on her knee, nor the sight up the sweep of her thighs, but the look in her eye—that contact had been far more exciting than any brush of their hands, more darkly intimate than a tongue.

Bowed over his feet in the darkness of the hallway he wondered at the new eccentricity of his body. Every part of him, each finger, each limb, was roaring.

She had run from him. Skim pictured himself as a reckless character, offering sexual escapades and a romantically difficult liaison. He sensed a corny grandness rising in his chest. What had stopped her?

He stood up, went to release a deafening urination, and returned to his room. He saw that Marek's bed was empty. "He must be upstairs with Gabriella." This unconsidered thought, interrupting his passionate speculations, calmed him down. The romance of Marek and Gabriella seemed

125

tame, ordinary. There was with them that undeniable proof of a mundane affection: indecision. It had been on, then off, with Marek's other loves in between, and now it was apparently on again. As for himself, he, Skim, had taken off like Cupid's arrow and was now traveling at such a speed that he felt in a weightless orbit of his own spectacular self. He got into bed without taking his clothes off. He might have to go upstairs at any moment. He might have to go out again.

In any case he could not sleep. Some time later (a time burning with the same questions repeated: What's happened to her before? Why did she run? What next?) he got up and wrote her a note. The missive told her frankly that she was richer to the taste than any praline, more beautiful to look at than meringue. He put it in an envelope and wrote her name on the front. After looking at it in his hand he tore it up.

Upstairs Julia had put herself to bed. She was calculating furiously. Part of him she could use? Physical desire was a tough sinewy thing attached from her sex to her brain.

Downstairs Skim was writing again, working up compliments with expensive triple chocolate brownies. The note would mark the beginning of a new life in a different emotional climate: saturated with passion and baking in its intensity. Was he trying to be too clever? Too keen? In fact it was she who was clever. She'd ignored him on the walk home. God how bright that made her! It was like quicksand under his feet, her cleverness. He might sink . . . He read the note and again tore it up.

The next morning he went to work with a restrained fury. It was tedious to have to work on the same thoughts until he could gather more.

TWENTY-FIVE

꩜

M AREK HAD GOOD reason to sleep even later than usual.
He and Gabriella, in their hours together upstairs, had
decided about themselves. She loved him. She had always
loved him, since their first meeting; she could remember
describing herself as complete after the knowledge of his
existence. She knew for certain she would love him forever,
whatever, as though he had been her own brother.

Marek, who had always before been looking for a sign,
found that such a thing wasn't necessary. He was convinced
that this was love because he had returned to it and because
now it felt like home. His other affections and flirtations
had all percolated away, distilling themselves into this one
concentrated version. They had already discussed the future. It had started as a sensible forecast, with him leaving
the Royal College of Music and their moving to Italy to find
jobs, but then it had disintegrated into a series of suggested
nicknames for the three boys and two girls, and how each
one in turn would have either his flaky skin between the
eyes or her old-looking neck, or both. Marek hadn't
wanted to stop—he suddenly felt, with ridiculous viru-
lence, like a child himself, of happiness, he concluded.

Once decided, they became quite dispassionate about consuming one another's virginity. They had sat side by side in the bed under a huge weight of blankets, holding hands and talking. They were sure they were going to do it. Neither of them knew what to expect. Pain, or pleasure, yes, but how much pain? What pleasure? Marek couldn't get out of his mind the slight worry of getting stuck in there. He'd once seen two dogs ending up pointed in opposite directions, painfully glued at the rear.

He and Gabriella kissed, sporadically, and shifted position very carefully, stopping frequently to talk. Then they laughed, and Marek thought he would lose it all together. Gabriella felt she was waiting like a dangerous Venus's-flytrap sort of animal. Both of them missed feeling excited, but carried on, slowly, almost as if they were two doctors offering themselves up for an important experiment.

Afterward they both commented on how surprisingly uneventful it had been.

"It just shows," said Marek, "what's here, how much is here." He pressed her against him, and watched her breast flattening against his chest.

"When we get used to it we'll go go go like rats in a sewer," she replied.

"But no laughing allowed," said Marek. "If there is laughing I can't go on."

"If I want to laugh?"

"You have to change it into something. Like a whoop."

When she fell asleep on his arm he looked down at her from on top of his propped elbow and remembered how they'd discussed this being the opening of adulthood. He imagined a wedding. She'd have the sun in her eyes outside on the church steps, and her dress would be painfully, brilliantly white to look at. She would be beautiful, undressed after a wedding. Then pregnant, and tired. Fatigue would be smudged under her eyes—she might be tetchy. How he'd struggle for money. Then, with small children, exhaustion for both of them would arrive like an unwanted guest. Their faces would begin to look different. Lines would appear. He looked closer at the pale wash of her face underneath him. Where would the lines be? There was the ghost of one between her heavy black eyebrows—there— he would chisel it in now himself, and sketch out the pattern of a few lines around her eyes. He'd be proud to finish her, to be responsible for this face until it stopped dead, suddenly declared complete, however old or young that might be. He liked to think of himself, privileged, adding detail.

He dropped down onto the pillows, careful not to disturb her. His body felt heavier than before.

Eventually he fell asleep, but later the same night they awoke to a slow realization of themselves. The unfamiliar bed heat of their bodies enticed them into a furious clinch.

Toward morning Marek crept downstairs in order to avoid Mrs. Gorse discovering them. As he descended in the dark he thought he might bump into her. She would be waiting for breath on a stair. He imagined the face on the statuette that Skim had made suddenly lighting up in front of him, like a Halloween mask. Gratefully he reached the ground floor and sought out the unused coolness of his sheets. He curled up, wrapping himself round an inner core of well-being.

TWENTY-SIX

⁂

Mrs. Gorse moved out of the house; it was a large-scale maneuver even though she'd be gone for only a month. She had her vehicle summoned to the front door, so an argument with a traffic policeman before breakfast kicked off the proceedings. She had two helpers, students found from somewhere. She had them bring things out: the typewriter, a big trunk full of something heavy, a series of travel suitcases.

"This way up, this way up," she ordered, thumping the heavy trunk as the procession passed by Santay's landing. The two washed-out youths carrying it were threatening to tip it sideways to get it up round the corner.

"It won't go," one of them claimed after some minutes of trying.

"That banister . . ." said the other.

"It went down like this," said Mrs. Gorse, lying, "now it goes up. Why not? You can't take the stairs to bits. Lift! Lift!"

They tried.

"Wait," she said, "put it down, down!"

She undid the buckles on the trunk and with a hurried movement she put an arm in and clamped a hold on

130

Hawkins who was just vacating a neat square hole among the books and papers. She scooped him up to her bosom. His legs stuck out; he looked like a chameleon clamped to a heaving black boulder.

"I have to be careful with him," said Mrs. Gorse. "No stress, that's why he was in there, in the dark. His hair is falling out. He is moulting."

The trunk could now be closed and tipped up whichever way necessary to get it out to the converted ice cream van which waited with its engine ticking at the bottom of the three steps. Mrs. Gorse was loaded in, an unorthodox package bound in tight black canvas.

Mrs. Gorse was lively on the journey, even her coughing was violent, and her laughs rudely meaningful. Her comments were sharp, but at the same time blunt and clumsy. Her manners veered from rigorous delicacy to animal coarseness. She made up rules for the two students, rules that were quite certain—lines written in her brow, which came down (*thunk!*) like a prison gate when she frowned her disapproval.

She was gone on the understanding that she would be returning every now and again, at least once a week, to check the progress of the electrician. Anyone in the building game had to be a crook and a liar.

The house dust, stirred up into the air by all this agitation, now settled: a fine gray fall. The empty rooms won back the charismatic echoes that had been displaced all this time by human occupation.

Gabriella went crazy. The sight of her employer disappearing drove her into a wild charge round the house. She whooped with freedom. She could do anything! Control had been taken away. She found herself scrabbling at one of Mrs. Gorse's notices taped to the wall in one of the bathrooms. The brittle sellotape came apart easily, leaving an ugly square stain—but there it was, an empty space. No orders, no commands. A brilliant light leapt in her eye.

131

Of course, Mrs. Gorse would be back in a month's time, but Gabriella flung this sensible thought out. She wanted to open a new, a different box of thoughts.

They explored Molly's room. Only a minimal glimpse of carpet and brown wall had ever been seen as she had always closed the door on her own unenviable privacy.

All her things, packed immaculately and covered with plastic dust sheets weighted around the edges, were still private and invisible, back to back in boxes, but her room—the cream and brown walls that had suffered her undressing in front of them countless times, the tall mirror that had witnessed the pale twin moons of her buttocks as she checked their shape—they stood there, available for inspection for the first time, mute, effaced by days of mundane unhappiness. "Be careful!" commanded Skim, seriously. They waited for him to continue. "Watch out for scabies."

Molly was an annoying loss for Santay. She had been his reliable source of help. He was left weakened. He didn't want to depend on anyone else. Dependency was too heavy, it crushed, people could only be forgiven for wanting to escape. Molly liked his weight on her. "Curiously sexual and disgusting," he murmured to himself.

After their first wandering scrutiny of her room, guilty in the absence of her permission, they took to having their evenings in there. It became a room common to them all. The floor became littered with their social apparatus: heaters, matches, ashtrays, mugs, candles, cushions, bottles, food, torches.

Skim was quite prepared to be involved when they were circulating their conversation just among the four of them, but he changed when Julia was there. She enchanted him—he became charged with his difficult ardor. When she came into the room he fell into an energetic silence. His interruptions—they seemed like interruptions then; never, as before, part of the general unfolding commentary—

132

came sporadically, and with a false vigor, that set the rest of them against him. He bullied objects: the ashtray, the wine bottles, the packaging on his sugary eats. He treated his own body recklessly.

Skim conspired to be alone with her. To have people there when they were in sight of each other was grotesque. Anyone else was trivial. He engineered for the two of them, and was careless as to how obvious were his machinations, but Julia was adept at avoiding his traps. Only when she wanted to did she allow herself to step neatly, gracefully in.

Skim had decided to pursue her story about the beetle. If he could use it to find out what he wanted to know, without giving away the fact that, at the moment, he knew nothing, then he would not risk her discovery of his ignorance. It annoyed him, not to be able to ask a plain question, having to turn everything he wanted to say into something with a beetle in it.

That fateful evening was spent in Molly's room, the carpet seeded with crumbs, wine bottles falling like skittles and butts crowding the ashtrays. It was pulled apart, slowly dismantled by people disappearing to their separate rooms.

Finally Julia tucked up her long skirt and allowed herself to sit on the stairs next to Skim. The bump to her bottom came as a comical sound in the darkness as she took her place. She expected his arm around her, but it didn't happen. She always felt pleasant after any surprise, however slight.

"Where've you been?" he asked, with a certain amount of accusation.

"Oh, I've been around."

"I've seen you," replied Skim, "but that's no bloody good!"

"Thank you very much."

"You know what I mean."

He loved the smell of her: powdery, clean. If he could soon touch . . .

"So how are you then, *Beetle?*" he asked, heavy-handed in his ambition for knowledge.

"Still swimming," she replied.

Skim's heart swelled. His penis stirred in its nest, beginning to put on a magical weight, encouraged by this message that coursed through his sexual system.

He couldn't think of anything more to say. He cast about for a way to take the story forward . . . the beetle in a bit of a state, swimming—what could he suggest? That it wouldn't drown? That dry land was close by?

Their candle died slowly at the bottom of its waxy grave. He said, "You might meet another beetle, you never know."

"A third beetle?" she asked.

"Yes, a third beetle . . ." said Skim, sampling this title for himself. He would be the tough, hard-backed flying beetle.

He said, "Keep swimming," to encourage her.

"Look." She took his hand and guided it to the fourth digit of her left hand. "No ring."

Skim stared through the darkness, as though trying to see her through a blanket. He hadn't realized that she'd been married. This was the information he'd been waiting for. No wonder she'd been reluctant to see him. The significance of their relationship suddenly became infinitely more profound. She'd left a fiancé or a husband because of him. Skim was awestruck.

Their hands stayed together. She felt the largeness, the volume of his against the delicacy of hers. She relished his physical scale. She wondered if the idea of the third beetle might not work after all. In Skim, in his casual manual profession, in his living of each day as though there was nothing much to think of beyond it, in his careless diet—in all this she saw an opportunity of getting her hands on an ideal exercise bike. She could expurgate her sex, which was threatening to make rules, to arrange her emotions along the axis of its own interest. She'd suffered already its closing-down of her rational affection for her husband. Skim might be a decoy, enough to confuse her sex, to put the monster to sleep and allow her to slip back behind the controls of her own brain. Perhaps she could isolate her sex and just accept a bloody good fuck once in a while. She laughed out loud at the obscene thought.

Skim put his arm round her shoulder. She slid her hand against his chest, and was pleasurably reminded of acres of hillside. She said, "I must go to the loo."

Skim waited in the dark, listening to the touch of her footsteps on the stairs. He felt scared. Would his body work? He took a deep suck of air. He couldn't reconcile how careful she was, and yet at the same time she seemed maddened, reckless. How quick her decisions.

She returned to sit next to him. He opted against jumping straight at her, for fear his nerves would make him clumsy. His body was too big. His thick fingers were heavy on her shoulders, and they might be too much for her breast or her face. He wanted to lie back, inert, and have her approach him . . . He would go into action only when she had worked herself up into a frenzy. He was gratifying himself with thought, before any possibility of failure. He recognized a soaring blood-sugar level. He could imagine Toblerone re-crystalizing in his brain. He started to move.

She felt his fingers move through the curtain of her hair and spread themselves on the back of her head. She turned and waited. His face loomed, and moved through the range of her focus to a blur. They opened their mouths to reach each other, and their guts stirred.

Now that she knew him a little better she said, "I've taken my pants off."

His hand drifted, and he found at the top of the run up her leg a bush, a tuft, or a very soft brush, or an animal's back.

He'd got it.

135

TWENTY-SEVEN

MAREK WAS SITTING in his favorite room at the Royal College, tapping his foot against the brown lino floor. Between his legs there was a viola. It was not his instrument, but he drew the bow slowly across F sharp, marking the note for as long as possible.

He had not done well in the end-of-term concert. His fingers had gotten lost on the keyboard. He'd hoped that the excitement would have screwed him up to a better performance than usual, but it had been worse. His mind had gone blank and his hands hadn't been able to gallop by themselves for long enough to cover for his mental blindness. When he'd gone up afterward to apologize, the composer had walked away from him, and no wonder, because his would have been a superlative achievement. To have created the sound, trained the musicians, and then controlled the scene with the baton . . . But it had been spoiled.

Marek liked the spectacle of music: the chorus of violins, the heroic percussion, the formal dress. It had a theatrical quality and people clapping was the essential aftermath. There was something about an audience's fervent applause: it was like they wanted to fit you up with a pair of wings and throw you aloft, to watch you fly for the first time. He could imagine doing almost anything for that feeling.

The applause had been polite. Perhaps he had been expecting too much.

He drew the bow back across the same note, moving it painstakingly slowly.

He had had too many distractions this term. The excitement of finding Gabriella had turned his concentration away from his studies. He needed to refresh himself, away from her. He wanted to rediscover his music.

He would embrace Gabriella and say, "I have to go home for Christmas." He would squeeze her hard and leave quickly. Their separation would earn them a delicious reunion.

He drew the bow back again. This note reminded him of his hometown. He'd been walking that time, and he'd noticed a set of telegraph wires stretched over the road in front of him; he couldn't remember them being there before, which showed how long he'd been away. He walked a little faster. When he'd next lifted his head he saw that a crow had landed on one of the wires directly over the road. It sat motionless, black, poised on the top line. It looked like a musical note. F sharp. He had hummed the note, steadily drawing on it. It set up a vibration of homeliness in him. Meanwhile he'd walked steadily onward, looking for any sign of movement from the bird. He could see none, not even a flick of its head. It maintained a faultless immobility. As he walked under the wires he'd felt a creeping-up of excitement and warmth, and a shrinking in size. The town could now welcome him; his portion of its secrets had suddenly become familiar again, freely given to him as part of the birthright of any of its sons. He had been signaled in by the crow.

He lifted the bow from the strings and waited, listening

137

until the note's call was lost. Yes, he ought to go home for a while.

SO, THE HOUSE hurtled toward Christmas. There were discomforts—the atmosphere of emptiness with those theatrical devices, doorways, just standing; the creep of the cold; the lack of hot water; no electric light; the to-ing and fro-ing with paraffin; the bullish, heavy gas cylinders—and all this made the activities of the few remaining tenants more feverish. They'd been distilled, pared down to a more essential version of themselves. They were determined to stay on during the rewiring, focusing on their own survival, bunkering themselves down in a concerted fashion. Skim collected pillows for himself from various rooms, and ransacked for extra blankets. He had three more music tapes—all choral works. Santay now ran two stoves in his large room, as well as a portable camping kit. The heaters burned longer, maintained by a steady trudging up the road with the red turbo containers.

They had doubled their money by not paying rent.

SANTAY DREW ON the cigarette. Brandy, food, book? This dismal queue of activities presented itself and he went along it, pickily, in fits and starts. All very well in theory, but a cigarette as soon as it was lit turned into a burning stick that made him feel sick and slow; brandy, if drunk alone, began biting back; food had become featureless, fiddly and dull; books—after so many books now he said to himself, "So what?" However, there was nothing else that could be stretched out to last beyond a minute.

All the things in the list had one aim in common—they all led toward sleep. Elusive, slippery, unattainable sleep.

It had always been the ultimate camouflage to hide be-

138

hind in the face of any trouble. Sleep! To sink gracefully . . . what happened under its spell could be beautiful or savage or absurd. It transformed his life from a painful tedium, a struggle to exist and coexist, into at worst a numb float through time, or at best an exhilarating, enigmatic ride round his own psyche.

There was a new one on his list, come to help out: a tranquilizer. He had a prescription. To be tired had been a privilege—perhaps he had misused it. Tiredness wasn't enough anymore to guarantee sleep. He'd discovered what had been lying just beyond his waiting and it was worse: this inescapable and ludicrous insomnia. He pictured the needle of an outsize syringe slipping under his skin, and if the plunge could soothingly deliver dreams . . .

"Come on brandy, in you go." He lifted his glass. "To Julia."

The photo of her pinned onto the board, its consistently friendly gaze, reminded him of how it used to be between them. Then he cursed himself for ever having allowed a quota of hope to creep into his idea of their relationship.

He was stuck here. Look how restricted were the possibilities now!

The three mountainous steps, a sheer rising height of an impossible number of inches, rejected any thought of escape.

The advertised accuracy of wristwatches in the Christmas magazines mocked the vagueness of his time, the absence of formal boundaries. If he could take forty winks here and there, that would be enough, he would have an internal clock, however eccentric its timekeeping.

This wakefulness and this tedious sorrow were increasing his preoccupation with the invisible deadline that would end his whole life. Death, yes it was a *dead*line, drifting back and forth, set somewhere in the future, but always closer. He was lying awake and listening for it, trying to see it coming. Like a late guest, it worried him.

Cigarette dabbed into the ashtray an unnecessary number of times; a gliding move (seated); a count of his resources; a return to blaming misfortune . . .

The slow disintegration of his windowsill (stupid that it affected his mood). The weather was eating anything that was left to it.

Where, or what would he be now, if . . . ? Looking out, and slightly up, he saw Marek appear, visible briefly in the squared frame of his own window as he packed to leave for Christmas. Skim, too, could be seen intermittently, wearing the headphones. Santay saw Marek take them off Skim's head and listen to check what it was. They spoke, but to Santay their mouths moved silently. Marek ducked and came up again, his neck and chest straining with the weight of something hanging off his arms. He moved forward, jerking the weight in front of him. How they moved, those two! Everywhere, without a thought.

Later Gabriella came to see him. He tried to shake himself into a receptive mood. She spoke about Marek for some time. She was worried . . . Santay nodded, swallowing the hurt of having no one to talk of.

"But you," said Gabriella, suddenly coming to attention. She'd been going on. "What you been up to today?"

"Me? I have made a model out of matchsticks."

"What, like a prisoner?"

"Yes, here it is. This box, you see, you slide it open, and there are matches inside. It's a model of a box of matches. Perfect in every detail."

There was a pause while she thought about this.

"Why you make this joke?" she asked, after it had fallen flat. Her brows dived into the middle, but she wasn't perplexed, she was mildly angry and tired of trying to jolly him.

"I don't know," he said.

140

She looked at him, her face blank, troubled at being asked for compassion.

"What a waste of a human being!" said Santay, rubbing his knees with his thumbs. His attempt at levity had been so transparently weak. "If only something would happen!"

TWENTY-EIGHT

◦❦◦

T HE ELECTRICIAN, A dapper man, worked even on Satur-
day mornings. He'd started upstairs in Gabriella's attic.
There were some traditional building noises: banging, muffled drilling, the clatter of lengths of wiring being thrown. A
bright yellow cable snaked up the stairs, carrying an emergency supply of power at low amperage for his tools. Inter-
spersed along its length were red plastic bulb-holders, some
of them complete with naked bulbs providing a working
light. It wound up round the banister like a colorful electric
beanstalk.

The last section of the stairs had been pulled apart, the
short floorboards leaning upright all the way to the top,
designed (it seemed to Gabriella as she climbed) to look like
broken piano keys in an absurd theatrical set. She was
remembering Marek's failure at the piano—she imagined
him sitting among the ruins.

She found herself lethargic with unhappiness, which
made every step more difficult than it was anyway. She
picked her way up, treading on the beams and the short
ends of floorboards still left in place.

In her kitchenette the electrician was heaving at a tail end of wire coming out of the wall. His effort seemed ridiculous.

Her own room was cold and abandoned. Its familiarity had been interrupted by odd possessions belonging to the electrician: a toolbag, a coat, and a pair of highly polished black shoes. She had to prevent herself from picking up something—anything—and breaking it, mangling it in her hands.

Did she really love Marek like a brother? "Who," she thought, "is betraying who?" Was she, in her uncertainty, betraying Marek, or was she disregarding love? But love was only a notion, an idea developed out of a long history of wishful thinking and ideal stories! She shrugged irritably. She didn't care about love. But then again, she admitted to herself as she made an exaggerated fall onto the bed, toppling herself like a tree felled or blown over, she cared more about love than anything else. She loved it.

Marek, his beautiful face, his floating personality, his confidence in her—was that trust now obsolete?

It was her fault; it was her mind that had not yet grown out of (or escaped from) the dreadful pattern that someone else, someone unknown, had drawn for it. There was a template for her somewhere, in that someone's workshop, and try as she may she couldn't turn herself out of true. This uncertainty about Marek could, if it ran beyond just a thinking thing, turn him into a victim. The thought was unbearable to her. She hated herself for not happily occupying the small circle described by his magical personality.

"What do I want?" she said out loud into the pillow which effectively muffled the words, but even so when she remembered the electrician next door she decided not to talk to herself again. He would think she was mad.

Daydreaming in the pillow, she put herself through a terrifying accident scenario. The car had rolled down the side of a mountain. She was stuck, hanging upside-down, looking through the rear screen. A wrong-way-up Skim

143

came scrambling down toward her, dodging the olive trees. She heard the window go, and felt the spray of broken glass on her legs. The car rocked, then the door flew open, and she felt his hands on her, releasing the belt, hauling her out, away from the vehicle. They ran, then stopped and turned, breathing hard. She reversed and leaned back against him. His arms went round—she saw the fingers lace together in front of her stomach. The car exploded into flames.

Afterward she had to laugh: a near-fatal car crash!? She was suspicious of herself on that score. She didn't even have a car. She measured the guilt like another new dress made out of the same cloth. Always a perfect fit. She was an old and practiced hand at that.

From the kitchenette came the sound of damage and the electrician's curse. Gabriella pushed herself up off the bed and went to look. She was aware that she'd appear scruffy and disheveled.

"Hell shitbag bastard," said the electrician in an uncharacteristic outburst, shouting directly at a pattern of bare wall from which the plaster had fallen, now arranged around his feet like a model earthquake scenario.

"Are you all right?" asked Gabriella.

"This place is rotten," he said, stepping backward out of the rubble.

She made a sound of sympathy and after a dutiful delay returned to her room. Now that she was on her feet again she would try to pull herself together. She began with a thorough scout around her possessions, hiding everything that might be damaged by dust under a cover on the bed, methodically putting to one side the few things that she would need downstairs. She gathered the alarm clock, her slippers, her bear (called Gently), and her letter-writing box.

She went downstairs and dumped her things in Molly's room.

Then, on an impulse, she went in to see Skim.

"Could I say you something . . ."

"What?" asked Skim, abruptly.

He'd been thinking of what Julia had said while sharply avoiding his grasp in the hallway. It had been—he could hardly *believe* it—a criticism of *him*. He was racked with worry because she'd not allowed him near her since. He felt like a cur, being punished. Yet he could remember her beneath him, spread like a delicacy.

"D'you think love can be perfect?" asked Gabriella.

"Yes," Skim blurted. He was about to get there, perfect love was within the scope of one last effort. Everything depended on the strength of his willpower, which he must prove to be a dominant force over Julia's—what? Her evasion? Her cowardice? No, her sensitivity, her carefulness, her wisdom.

"I'm not so sure," said Gabriella.

"If you're in love, you're in love, and that's it."

"Is it?"

"Yes."

Gabriella hated Skim at that moment. His look, thrown sideways but still directly, and of an accusing length, demeaned her. She suffered under his judgment because she partly agreed with him.

"Sometimes I'm thinking," she said, "that I am a sister to Marek, that's like brother and sister."

"When?" asked Skim.

"When what?"

"When do you feel that," demanded Skim, "when *exactly*? Is it when he comes to you in bed?"

Gabriella winced. She didn't know that she could feel miserable so suddenly.

"Is important?" she asked.

"I think so."

"Why?"

"Because then you don't have love for him, not in your guts."

"No love?" asked Gabriella, considering this numbing possibility not for the first time.

"Well . . ." Skim shrugged. He was being cruel. It occurred to him to wipe his mouth.

Gabriella felt that her consultation had come to an end. It briefly crossed her mind to offer him money for his advice. She left the room.

DARKNESS FELL. SKIM dashed off a visit to the crowded late-night Italian shop over in the mews and then returned to settle in his bed, dissolving slabs of chocolate in the roof of his mouth.

The candle was running out again.

With his gums stinging from the sugar, he got up to replace it, pressing the wax stick into the little clay holder that Marek had made. He tried to move quietly, although he was aware that Gabriella wasn't yet asleep (she had opted for Marek's bed, thankful for his smell, wishing for sleep).

Skim worked on his idea of Julia, building his conception of her by laying down in his head enough times certain opinions: that she was wise, that she was far-sighted, that she didn't live from day to day, that she was timid and sensitive and therefore required him to look after her.

His eyes and ears patrolled for sight or sound of her return. He made detailed plans . . .

By the side of his bed sat a bowl and a spoon, permanently on standby to be used for ice cream. Once in a while it was given a clean, but mostly it was like a dog's bowl, so constantly used and emptied as to keep it from going off. On his pillow the cassette turned laboriously in the cheap machine. He followed different strands in the interwoven voices. He was moving deeper into music. It was accumulating in him.

When he next looked over to Gabriella, she'd turned to

lie on her back, and her eyes were open. He was about to say something but he stopped himself, and—it was marvelous, he counted it as Julia's influence—he actually *thought* about what he was going to say.

He put suggestions to himself: "Are you awake?" . . . "What are you thinking?" . . . "D'you want to talk?" . . . but, as he rejected all of them, he began instead to burn a slow fuse of anger. He hadn't previously been given to thinking before speaking, why should he start now? He wanted to get back to Marek, to his influence, so he turned the music off and asked Gabriella, "What happens when you're dead?"

Gabriella stirred. After a pause she replied, "Maybe heaven, I don' know."

"Anyone who dies ought to do it properly, ought to be bollock-liftingly frightened, leaping into nothing."

"No one die like that, do they?"

"I would," replied Skim, "I'm going to shit myself and die groveling in panic."

"You are very righteous," said Gabriella, fond of him, and powerfully grateful to have a feeling different from the boredom she'd been stuck with all day.

"Righteous?" said Skim, "that's the last thing I am."

"It's the first thing."

"Always right, true, but never righteous."

The laugh made Gabriella feel extraordinary, as though her blood had stopped and reversed direction.

She began to talk, at ease in her one and only lover's bed, with Skim lying just over the other side.

Skim's work jeans were lying there, as though to mark out the last position of a dead man. She noticed that the belt had a vulgar buckle, lying open. Skim's sexuality had escaped from there; it was still somewhere in the room, she thought.

Skim blew out the candles, but left the stove burning. It spilled a steady, glowing light, uninterrupted by drafts.

147

He was still lying in wait for the sound that would mean Julia's return to the house. Should he go up and demand attention when she came back? No. He had to stop himself from that. What was her problem? If only . . . His exclusion from her life was like a door slammed in his face, and the world, outside of her world, was infinitely more cheerless than it had been before.

He wondered what she would be doing for Christmas.

When the tape had run to the end of its second side he removed the earphones from his ears. He wanted even more music, he had a thirst for it. Yet he could not choose without Marek. Just pick a new piece out of a hat? It might ruin everything. Marek's suggestions had become a ritual, and each cassette so far had been perfect: accessible, but complex enough for him to look for further discoveries within it. Both he and Gabriella needed Marek, he realized with a mild envy.

"Have you rung Marek?" he asked, having checked that Gabriella's eyes were open.

"No," she replied, "I did not."

"Does his family know about you?" asked Skim.

"Oh yes. They look at me, and they waiting, and very pleased."

"Why pleased?"

"Catholic family."

Skim felt the familiar lurch of displeasure, but he didn't speak. Nobody should be held responsible for their own parents.

Skim reflected that he had been ignoring himself since meeting Julia. His individuality was under threat—from himself. He was trying to give it away. Marek, he needed to be back with Marek to get himself back. He had been neglecting Marek.

"D'you know what Julia told me?" he asked.

"What?"

"She said I only lived for the present."

"What else can you do?"

"I don't bloody know. What d'you think she meant? She said it like an accusation. I mean, what have I done wrong, for God's sake? She still hardly knows me, but she accuses me of only living from day to day. What does she do? Live a week at a time? For God's sake! You can't help but live from one second to another. It's like a conveyor belt! What does she want?"

Both Skim and Gabriella were preoccupied at that moment with the inspection of a surprising internal damage.

Skim saw himself as wrong-footed, clumsy, unclever. He had proof. It came from a small but significant memory: when Julia had first walked into their room, she had pointed at one or two things—the battery-powered effigy of Mrs. Gorse in the box, the candles burning—and she'd said, "It's like something out of Dickens."

He'd replied, "*Wuthering Heights*."

She had recently revealed to him by accident (one of those accidents that teach you something) that *Wuthering Heights* had been written by someone else. He remembered her original silence when he'd made the gaffe and it was far worse a thing than a comment or a laugh given at the time. He felt stupid, and her small cleverness seemed condescending to him. He wanted to rip through all this "third beetle" stuff, this riddle of a relationship. He wanted to grab her and say he loved . . .

But then her face would drop in disappointment, empty of expression, and again he would not have been agile enough. She needed catching! Every sentence had to do it.

Click—there it was. He could hear the sweep of her clothes.

SANTAY ALSO HEARD Julia's key in the door, and the soft night tread as she went upstairs. Then, a short while later, came the heavier bumps of Skim's feet and the low grumble of his voice as they talked up on the first floor. Santay groaned. If he'd been asleep he would have missed this.

He dragged in the sickness of another cigarette, but exhaled fast. He blew the stream of smoke hard, continuing until his lungs bottomed out, empty, then he closed his throat, holding it. His chest ached. He looked at the smoldering tip, and the thin, sophisticated poison, steadily lifting. Smoke signals. Saying what: "Wait"? He allowed himself to suck air; his chest billowed, full.

There they were, upstairs above him. What were they doing? Would there be noises? He stood the live end of the cigarette on his knee and watched the trouser cloth glow and creep back to accommodate the incandescence. He pushed the stub down, hard. A grunt came to his throat and he began to pant, rocking back and forth. Soft moans came, a rising scale on the outward breaths. Still rowing, and with the groans coming faster, he tipped his head back and closed his eyes, then slumped to an exaggerated stillness in his chair.

He began to giggle, but it wasn't funny: it had a nasty twist in its tail, like the sort of giggle you'd find under a stone.

The cigarette smoke had filmed his eye during that bit of self-pity. What with that, and the brandy warming him . . . He lifted a tear onto his knuckle and sipped it.

JULIA EXPECTED SKIM to be everywhere now—in between the sheets as she peeled them back to climb in, behind the bathroom door, under her towel, hiding ready to pop out of the box when she went to find clothes, so it was no surprise to hear him coming after her.

Skim couldn't see her; the room was still in darkness. Then came the rasp of a lighter and the single strand of fire leapt and stood cosily in her hand. She walked here and there in the room, dipping to feed candles. Skim admired

150

the warmth thrown on her face by each one as it took the flame from her. She stood upright and turned toward him, but her eye was snagged on the way.

"Agh!" she exclaimed in astonishment.

"D'you like them?" asked Skim.

"What are they?"

"They come from an old children's show. Years ago. Jerry brought them over for me in the van."

"God they're huge."

"D'you like Beatrix Potter?"

"I like Beatrix Potter, yes," she said, ambiguously.

Two life-size animal dummies sat one in each chair, made out of hessian, stuffed with rags. Their expressions were aloof, but with a point of funniness going on, so they looked secretive.

(One was looking at him, Skim noticed.)

"What are you doing for Christmas?" Skim asked, tucking the tips of his fingers into his pockets.

(Was the dummy laughing? If he lifted his hand to his ears he might find straw poking out.)

"I hate Christmas," said Julia. "Like most people."

"Come with me," said Skim cheerfully. "Three of us are in a cottage near Worthing. Stay as long as you want."

"No," answered Julia, "I'd better go home for the day."

"Where's home?"

"Barnes."

"Well, why don't you—" began Skim, but he heard a tinge of complaint in his voice, so he started again, trying to make it sound like an adventure: "Why not blow them out? Sneak away with me for a night, and go home later."

"Can I say maybe?" asked Julia politely.

"I'm going by train." Skim took one step at a time toward her. "Christmas Eve, six-thirty-six. Victoria. Meet me by Platform 9."

He was close enough. He took her huge buttoned coat in his arms. She was under there somewhere.

151

"No . . ." She had her hands pressed on his chest. Skim released her quickly. "I'll write it down for you," he said, retreating fast now toward the door, as if he had a purpose for leaving.

"OK," she replied, and turned away so he'd be encouraged to close the door instead of look at her.

"OK!" Skim repeated to himself as he trotted down the stairs, "OK!"

TWENTY-NINE

THE STUDENT WATCHED, bewildered and hungry.

Mrs. Gorse took a handful of potatoes and without cere-mony dropped them onto the four-squared surface of the cooker.

"I only invite people I approve of," she said. "You are to be honored."

"I . . ." began the student, but she stopped to watch Mrs. Gorse, who was walking *backward*—with careless proficiency—toward the sink. There she took a clean saucepan, scrubbed it briefly, then rested it all anyhow on top of the potatoes. Its handle pointed accusingly at her head.

"I'm not mad, you understand?" Mrs. Gorse was speak-ing to the saucepan.

"No, no," came from behind her. The student, eager for approbation. Mrs. Gorse hauled herself around.

"No one can write me off. They are stupid if they do. It is their loss. I am just at a time of life. An exciting time, if you must know."

"Oh?"

"But you won't know. How could you? Young people

153

today think life is a cinema they're in. It's the fault of motor cars, and everyone wearing too many spectacles. Always looking at the world through a screen."

The student made a start on several conversations but Mrs. Gorse didn't appear to hear her.

After a while Mrs. Gorse took a potato, unseating the saucepan still further, and cut twice into its spongy body. She stood by the sink and began to rub the mud off each quarter with her thumbs.

She muttered, "Chaos," and then stopped abruptly. A drip from the tap sanely counted the pause. "Hawkins!" she said, dropping everything and rushing outside. The student followed.

Mrs. Gorse was standing on the pavement, looking both ways.

"Hawkins!" she shouted, urgently.

A neighbor opened the window and called out to the boulder-like figure standing on the pavement outside.

"Please," said the neighbor, "it's after midnight. Can't it wait until morning?"

"It's my cat," shouted Mrs. Gorse, "Hawkins. He has disappeared. Have you seen him? Black, with a white thing. I must find him. He will be squashed flat. In Chapel Street he knew the pedestrian crossings. Here he is a stranger."

The sound of the window sliding shut coincided with her call, "Hawkins!" Two policemen, professionally interested in the slam of the window and the urgency of her tone, turned toward her.

"Are we all right, madam?"

"We? Who's 'we'?"

"Can I ask if you live near here?"

"I don't know . . ."

"There seems to be some confusion." They looked at the student, waiting for help with this woman. The student didn't know what to do without being ticked off by someone, so she waited.

"Yes, yes..." Mrs. Gorse looked at her feet. "Hawkins!"

"May I ask your name?"

"What?" asked Mrs. Gorse, rocking from side to side in agitation, staring at each boy policeman in turn. "What?"

"Your name?"

"My name, what is my name?" Then she demanded, "Where are your manners?"

"We want to help, madam."

"My name?"

"Yes."

"I can't remember. I...I..."

"D'you live here?" asked Police Constable Townsend.

She frowned, and looked at each one in turn. She waved her hand. They might have been moths attracted by the light of her doorway. "Don't bother me. Please leave. I've had enough of your conversation."

She turned indoors, followed by the student.

THIRTY

DAYLIGHT, WHEN IT came, was no more than darkness diluted. The light couldn't get through. It was carried in the clouds, and lowered down by rain onto the windows of the house.

There was no sign of the electrician. Several clues gave evidence that he had withdrawn for Christmas: the yellow plastic supply cable had gone, likewise the overalls that were usually draped in a neat curve over a box at the foot of the stairs.

The dead-rat smell of house dust! It resulted in small nodules of black appearing on Santay's blasted handkerchief.

The window in his room swam with damp, and the glass was brittle underneath. He thought he would get a visit from Gabriella; if she woke she would come and seek him out. There would be hours of talking and paraffin fumes and bad toast from the stove.

But first it was Julia, who had now started her Christmas holiday. She knocked, and came in very gently. She apologized for not having come to see him for a day or two. She explained that she'd needed some time to herself. To Santay this was like holding a red rag to a bull. Kneading his scrapped knees with both hands, he asked, "What's up?"

She was standing facing him when he asked, with her hands behind her back, standing in a soldier's state of attention. Her mysterious pornographic tits stood proudly like buns in the air above him. She seemed surprised and delighted by his question.

"God!" she exclaimed.

"What?" he asked.

"That *you* should ask that," she replied. Julia thought that people *knew* without having it spelled out for them. This implied that she always *knew*, of course, without being told. She turned away from Santay and began fastidiously picking at the papers pinned on his board.

She said, "I can't bear it though, how everything is always so deliberately difficult. I mean, I don't mind that things aren't simple, and cut and dried, but I do mind when every situation you come across is deliberately perverse, and when you yourself are caught up in it against your will. I don't mind the effort, it's the impossibility of any answer, of *any* resolving of *any* situation at all, that's what kills me."

"Give me an example."

"Well if there were any justice it should be impossible to fall in love with someone who isn't in love with you. But it's what always happens. No wonder the triangles are eternal! Such a piled-up mess! Sex and children and money and vanity and power . . . I just want to cancel, I don't want any of it, no choices, no opportunities, no desires or achievements! It's all so . . ." she struggled, looking up at the ceiling and giving a short groan of frustration before continuing, "it's all so untidy. Untidy! Badly organized! It's bloody unfair!"

"You're talking about Skim?" asked Santay. The walls peeled back; the floor dropped away.

He heard her words: "No. Yes. I mean not really. He is a side issue . . ."

Santay sat there, the emptiness nudging at his throat from below. What should he do? Pinch himself? Change the subject?

She took his hand when she saw he was struggling for control.

Santay had to explain his grief somehow. "I'm sorry, it's just . . . it's just I can't shake off the idea of dying. It's invaded the place . . . the whole atmosphere . . . I . . ."

They waited while he recovered.

"I feel selfish," said Julia, staring at Santay as he put the slow, slow kettle on the Calor ring.

"Why?"

"Because I have been ignoring you on purpose yet you've been kind to me. I'm just on the surface of these events, aren't I? I don't belong . . ."

"Nonsense. You've fitted in."

"I need time to myself, more than anything. I've been trying to snatch it, wherever I can get it. Blown that now, anyway."

"How's that?" he asked greedily.

She slowly edged away from him, in some discomfort, but her embarrassment was conveyed by her back as she scoured his pin-board.

"D'you think you were the same person, then?" she asked, pointing at the photo of him with the bulbous red motorcycle between his legs.

"No, I was alive, then. I'm halfway to dead now."

"Don't!" she exclaimed, genuinely angry. She waited. Everything waited. The empty mugs. The photo stuck in a flash of light. Santay, still waiting.

Then she asked, "Who were you in love with?"

"My own good self, I expect. I had a passionate desire to fiddle with some girls, but nothing serious. I wasn't old enough to be serious."

Santay wheeled himself over to the tea-making equipment and set himself going on the old routine. They drank the hot liquid, companions.

When she left the room it was after a very quiet and quick goodbye which came out riding on her breath against his cheek. There had been no kiss on the corner of his mouth.

A COLD HAD settled on Santay's chest, exacerbated by the cigarettes. Each breath felt like it disturbed only the top layer of a stagnant reservoir of smoke that had been in there for years. Idly, he tried to think of an exercise to get his veins in use, to get some heat to his skin to throw off the cold, to get himself tired.

His bed, that favored place where he had previously been able to go for all peace and adventure and warmth, now lay there in the corner of the room like an inanimate slab used for torture. Perhaps he could take some practical measures to improve things. The mattress buttons stuck through into his shoulders, for instance: he could do something about that. Laboriously, embarking on what he knew would be a long but worthwhile project, he dragged the bedding off, and taped over the buttons with vinyl tape. He tied the underblanket properly, circling from one side to the other. Layer followed on layer.

He continued until it looked perfectly made, like in the hospital. Fussing over his bed, it occurred to him that he was behaving like a decrepit old family pet.

THIRTY-ONE

SKIM WAS SITTING on an abrasive concrete seat opposite Platform 9, restlessly checking any one of three different clocks. In his hand he held two tickets for the 18:36. The train stood heavily poised for the off, aiming down the tracks. He had decided to buy for both of them when Julia hadn't arrived and there was only a quarter of an hour to go before departure. Between his feet was a bag; it denoted him as traveler, one of the long-distance crowd, not a commuter. In front of him, above the timetable, the right-hand number of the digital clock blinked and showed the beginning of a fresh minute.

It was Christmas Eve, and thousands spilled onto the station concourse. Skim's gaze cruised over the faces of the crowd, picking out young females, discarding them, waiting for sight of Julia. He was still more or less at ease, waiting.

If she was here they'd be smiling, finding the right carriage, searching for seats . . .

Why no Julia?

Eleven minutes left. He considered this: should he expect

her to pay for her own ticket, or should he just say nothing and leave it up to her?

When the clock winked again he sprang to his feet to trawl through the crowd. He was pleased that people got out of his way. He expected them to. He was carried along into an imitation of his own importance. There was only one other person in this concourse who mattered. He searched through as many people as he could, rejecting them all, and then (quickly, because time was running out) he moved away from the main areas to visit the obscure corners of the station concourse where she might have got washed up by the running tide of travelers.

When he had completed this wider search he turned back in the direction of their meeting place with a sudden rush of willingness. He felt proud to have neatly reversed the position: *she* would now be waiting for *him*!

But she might be worried, standing by the barrier, so he accelerated, walking on his toes to see a clear path through the crawling mess of people. Next to him, sometimes behind him, he pulled at his bag (stuffed with clothes, all clean). Why did people keep bumping into it, the clumsies?

Approaching the platform barrier he ransacked the masses for a spare female who would be floating, more uncertain than the rest, but there was none. Everyone was walking through, sure of their purpose, conniving to get the least bothersome seat possible—while he had to wait.

He checked: five minutes.

Suddenly he heard a voice telling him, "Relax, buddy!" He turned round to see a man's face, sprung with sweat, grinning at him. There was a raised arm (it looked almost too heavy to lift), and a finger wagging on the end of it.

"Don't have a heart attack," the man said authoritatively, "over a late dame!"

Skim turned away, muttering under his breath. No wonder the fat fool was used to waiting.

161

He went to check the anxious ribbons of people shunting up to the ticket windows. Behind him another minute flicked forward to take the place of the last one.

No Julia.

He returned to the barrier, taking up a position in close proximity to the ticket inspector. He felt a calmness gathering. If there were only two minutes to go, then he would be seeing Julia, at the latest, in two minutes' time. A sensation of warm privilege stole over him. The moment of their meeting was coming closer, it couldn't escape him, it was squeezed in a trap. He imagined, in the fast-approaching last minute, their meeting at the barrier, and their dash to get to the waiting train. He pictured himself having to knock the barrier guard aside with an elbow, hurrying with Julia, catching the train as it moved. Through clenched teeth he muttered a message to her, "Come on!"

She wouldn't be running, even having been stuck in a bus or a tube tunnel. She would stroll up, cool as usual, blind to his anger, and then he wouldn't be able to be angry, he'd bite it back, he'd eat up all the anger himself.

She would read a book in the train, he realized.

"I don't mind," he said to himself. "Anything!"

Fraudulent people (they weren't her) were running toward him, their looks seeking the open doors along the platform. He felt charged with an electrifying tension; it was almost enough to make him move off along the gleaming twin tracks himself, away from this ordinary event of such unparalleled importance. He had a sudden wish to climb up and slam his hand against the faintly audible clock above him and hold it there until Julia struggled free of her delay.

With no awareness of the damnation of the moment the barrier guard closed the gate, and the platform official, with the whistle held ready in his mouth, swung the last door shut (the slam hurt Skim's whole life) and, looking up and down the length of the sleekly articulated carriages, gave a shrill whistle, commanding the train to move off deliberately without Skim and Julia.

A succession of different questions fought for nonexistent answers. What had happened to her? Was it deliberate? Should he go home, check hospitals? Dejected and furious, it was only left to him to find the time of the next train, and settle down to wait for that. It was pointless to move about looking all over the place. "Careless bitch!" Skim thought to himself, looking down into his lap and fanning out the two train tickets: they were a hand of cards, a bum deal that had cost him half a week's wages. If she didn't come it would be humiliating. He'd have to queue up to reclaim his money.

The people washed over him, irritating him with their chatter, their muddled footsteps, their smell, their tidy clothes, their soppy Christmas-holiday excitement, their panic.

Then suddenly, "God, if she's hurt!"

He sank into a more settled grieving, surrounded by the diesel-munching trains, one eye fixed to the transfer of each number on the clock.

THIRTY-TWO

⚜

M<small>RS. GORSE WAS</small> wrapping Christmas presents. She liked to bury her head in practical tasks, what with these walls. Brown! The color of mud, cardboard boxes, dirt, old meat. She would decorate.

She had no lists. Names tumbled with each object that she picked up, then one would stick and she'd write on the wrapping paper. A Christmas message, and the name large for her convenience.

The old telephone bared itself among the pile of other presents, its plastic vulgarly faded. She was pleased—she had managed to get hold of a plug for it. She put it in a shoebox and taped it into a brown-paper jacket.

Expressions no longer jousted across her face to knock each other down. She held the box aloft triumphantly.

Santay!

She was an old woman now, allowed ease. "I don't want to be young," she thought. "I am alone, a forgetful old wrinkled woman, I wouldn't want that business of youth again. They are led by their penises, and by their tits, the young. They stick them out and follow them. No wonder they are worried whether these things are big enough."

She found that the words were coming out into the beige air of the flat, they weren't thoughts at all. She was talking to herself. She began to laugh aloud, looking down at her chest. "Mine are pointing at the ground," she said. "No good following them! God, I'm mad, am I?"

THIRTY-THREE

SKIM STRODE ROUND the perimeter of the station building, itching to kick the pigeons. A worse mood had come on him. He thought about roses representing love. The cliché worked. He understood the thorns: they were tearing him on the inside. He saw the rudeness of the flower and its bloody color. "Clichés only become clichés," he thought, bitterly, "when they are true often enough."

He wondered if that was a cliché.

It depressed him to be back sitting on the same cold concrete seat as before. He was grateful that the sweating man had gone, but jealous of his departure.

When the 21:45 train had snaked slowly out of the station, he stood up in a sick mood, in dread. She'd been killed by a car . . . As he reached his full height he stopped and looked around wildly. He'd lost his bag. He swore, but then immediately cast off the loss, mentally throwing the missing bag away from him as far as possible—he did it with a curse and a kick in his lengthening stride. He patted his two thighs, his buttocks, his chest—money?

After wasting half a dozen calls on the public phone he was told of a girl, an attempted suicide with long brown

166

hair, well dressed, who had as yet not been identified. He tore the page out of the directory and set off at a trot toward the hospital. He knew it was her. His urgency fed on itself and increased as he ran. He didn't care about the bag.

He hailed a cab. Locked inside the plastic interior with its grab handles and formal notices about smoking and safety, he realized that he'd never been in one before. There was a small printed sign: FOR YOUR COMFORT AND SAFETY PLEASE SIT BACK IN THE SEAT.

He leaned forward, as if that might get him there faster. He had other signs made up: THANK YOU FOR NOT BEING ANGRY and PLEASE DON'T BE SAD and NEVER GET SPURNED.

He ended up waiting for permission in a cold, hard room. Somewhere in the giant all-night laboratory of health was the girl. Julia's suffering should be this massively important and expensive, he thought. When he was called to identify her he saw that it wasn't Julia.

Outside the hospital, he waited for any sense of direction to come to him. Where was he?

Lost.

The night was far from black this close to the ground. There was a mood of celebration given off by the harshly accelerating cars. This public happiness was unfair to Skim. He tramped the streets, turning always in the best direction, as far as he could guess it, for home. He was exhausted, and, perhaps for the first time, he felt genuinely (it was bewildering, this) stupid. Of course she had stood him up. Just like she had always stood him up. His run to the hospital seemed naïve; more money had been wasted.

"What is the most you can think about someone?" Skim's stride became longer as he asked himself. He was trying to shake her off. He couldn't see his way through the density of his thoughts about Julia. He thumped his chest hard. Nobody else but Julia in there. Thoughts about her manned the pumps, her voice sprang the valves, her small hands wielded the mechanical gizmos of his heart. She had him hung on a hook with her name on it.

Yet Marek had *pretended* to be in love all the time with those different girls. "And now Gabriella," he thought, angry. He pounded the pavement heavily with his feet and puffed out his chest, trying to feel as confident as before, making his way among the big, unfamiliar, shut-down buildings.

He was going to have a problem getting back into the house. The keys had been in his stolen bag. It crossed his mind to blame Julia for his humiliating return. He would have to pound on the door. Gabriella would see failed, damaged goods. Walking the streets he looked for coins in the gutter and imagined finding a suitcase stuffed with money.

THIRTY-FOUR

GABRIELLA AND SANTAY were doing their best. Her eyes looked smudged, worn out, Santay thought. He suggested that they might forget about any celebration, there being only two of them, but she wanted to get drunk.

Santay held a lager in one hand, in the other a brandy. Each arm in turn lifted. It was, after all, nearly Christmas Day.

Gabriella had wine in her glass, and her eyebrows came together in a clash of distaste every time she took it down. She had a leaden cold—if she wasn't swallowing the liquid going in she was wiping up what was coming out. She was aiming to get blasted.

She shut her eyes, and her good looks disappeared.

Santay asked, "Have you heard from Marek?"

"He phoned, yesterday. He send his love. I just shout that I miss him. Seems so far away, now."

"He's coming back."

"Yes."

"I know you've been unhappy with him," said Santay.

"No unhappy. Unsure. I love him, but my heart is so false. *My* heart, and is false to *me*! Perhaps I should tell him."

"Yes, tell him."

"I talk with Skim," she said, and she related Skim's offhand denunciation of her feelings. Her eyes circled around the cornices, across the boarded fireplace, over the coverings on Santay's bed, the line of her sight cruising here and there like an insect flying arbitrarily, blindly exploring the room. In a similar manner her thoughts were picking over the workings of her life. She stared into her acid wine. She could see Marek, she could *see* him like no one, nowhere, never before in her life. The smoothest skin was on his brow, underneath the fringe. It had been hidden away, saved from wear. His moustache—the hairs were like a soft brush for the back of her neck! She loved his smile which lifted evenly on both sides of his face. In the morning he woke up so slowly. He raised his head like he'd just been saved from a drowning. And the effort! His shoulders drooped with the weight of each muddy awakening. His eyes were slow, and a bruised strangeness in his aspect made him look ready to be hurt by the first thing he might see. Only slowly did the dreariness dissolve away, and his face would freshen to its normal repose of innocence and good humor, and his body (the fingers like rubber on the piano) move up to its waking speed.

Gabriella and Santay just sat, happy to be drunk in their paraffin-heated isolation from the outside, where the streets lay deserted, empty of those hurrying, spending pedestrians who had all vanished, gone home to act the family. Most of them were in bed by now. They were left behind, these two invisibles, in their abandoned patch.

The phone surprised them.

Gabriella got up, staggering slightly on her horsey legs (they moved like ceaseless engines, thought Santay). He could hear her voice pattern being interrupted in mid-flow out in the hallway.

"Mrs. Gorse," she said when she returned.

"So late. Amazing." Santay was incredulous. "What did she say?"

"I pick up the phone," began Gabriella, "and she said, immediately, 'Who's there, who's there,' like she's in a dark room with a burglar. I say it was me and she says, 'I know I know that's you, but who else is there? Who's there now?' I say just me and Santay for Christmas, Marek coming back after, and Skim, and Julia, then everyone else when the electricity is finished. She just said 'Happy Christmas' three times and that's it."

"Strange woman," said Santay.

Then Gabriella was crying a bit (affected by the drink) and sporadically fitting in a smile between inhaled slugs of breath. She shook her head in disbelief at such serious inland slippage. Her family was miles away. She felt alone.

Later she kissed him and left, tottering on her feet. When she turned for a final wave Santay was parked there among the shadows in his room. "Happy Christmas," she said, as she slid out of sight behind the door, drawing it behind her. Santay was left with the scuff against the loose rug, and the click.

As usual he waited until there was no chance that she might return before starting. Then, still partly clothed, he hauled himself onto the bed. He was like a somnambulant man drowning in wakefulness, trying to save himself. The night was a gaping hole.

Cigarette, more brandy, aiming for daylight.

GABRIELLA RETURNED TO Skim and Marek's room, and without taking off more than her shoes and cardigan she found her old place in Marek's bed. She blew out the candle. It would be easier to find memories of Marek in the dark.

Her eyes closed eventually, while images skidded wildly across the forefront of her consciousness: disjointed,

171

panicky scenes, concocted somehow in primitive brain-scope: it was a face talking, but the lips were missing; people being killed off in a foreign country. Mrs. Gorse appeared, some way off, planting herself squarely in front of her and waving. A baby dangled, suspended from her bosom. The figure receded rapidly. Gabriella felt a lurch of anxiety.

SKIM TURNED AND turned again toward Chapel Street, ready to barge his way into the house. He was in a new class: under-dog; and more specifically, an underdog padding through the streets knowing it has a sign on its forehead saying UNDER-DOG. It was working cruelly on him. Even if he wasn't a dog he was a guinea pig in an unwholesome psy-chological experiment which someone outside of himself, a mysterious controller or torturer, had put into effect.

"It's bloody God, isn't it, that's who," said Skim, mutter-ing the words out loud while the wallop of his feet slowed and stopped outside the house.

"If people are going to believe in God," continued Skim, looking at the front door and talking to the whole world, "then why can't they realize that he's an evil fucking bas-tard?"

He was searching the blank face of the building, trying to find a way in. Behind the front railings a set of narrow steps led down to the basement entrance, and he descended in the hope of finding an open window. They were all closed tight, the joints painted over; Mrs. Gorse hadn't opened them for years. He tried the door down there, but it was locked. He was stuck outside. He'd have to use the bell and wake them all up.

(GABRIELLA'S EYELIDS FLICKERED. She was in a tunnel, star-ing at the expressionless face of a disaster. The alarm had gone off . . . Her tongue explored the inside of her mouth.

172

Why were the teeth coming loose? They began to drop out as she touched them with her tongue. More and more came loose and fell. An impossible number of teeth flooded her mouth. She was losing them down her chin. It was continual work.)

SKIM HAD KICKED his heels for long enough. Nobody was showing up. He'd get arrested, hanging about. No keys! Emasculated, impoverished, and locked out by Julia.

He returned down the steps to the basement entrance. Safely hidden from any casual observer, he raised a foot and rammed it against the door. He saw a slight give.

He struck again, harder, determined.

GABRIELLA WOKE UP.

She was still feeling for the edges of her mouth. When she heard the second thud from downstairs the unfathomable fear of a bad dream mixed seamlessly, immediately, with real alarm as she recognized the unmistakable sound of someone breaking in. She froze in her bed, startled by the sudden movement in her heart—a thudding. It seemed medically dangerous.

She noticed the carelessness of the noises down in the basement. The confidence of the intruder confirmed her inability to do anything but wait, propped up on an elbow with a nervous shake in it, straining her ears for more information. Should she run now? She had most of her clothes on. Where to? If she went out of the door she'd be running toward the intruder. She didn't have time to find her keys and get out. It was too late to run upstairs—the man, arms like hydraulic tools, might be outside her door right now (but he might not).

She'd have to go. Now or never. She drew back her bedding (slowly, quietly) and put her feet on the floor, pausing to listen. Still no sound. She stood up and headed for the door.

Suddenly a light came on. The fact that it was *electric* light increased her shock; she was frozen except for her head which swiveled in a lightning, puppet-like motion to check the source. As she did so the light went out. The mute figurine of Mrs. Gorse had been illuminated, just for a moment. It left a dying impression on her retina. Gabriella leapt back into bed, barely able to control the combination of terrified keenness and disabling clumsiness that afflicted her actions. She buried herself, and restrained her breathing in order to be able to listen. She could hope that the footsteps would pass by her door . . . She heard the approaching feet climb the last three stairs and then stop. She pressed her head into the pillow and clamped her eyes shut. She whispered a curse. Marshaling her jittery breath, ordering calmness, she set herself to a breathing pattern that would convincingly feign sleep, opening her mouth an inch against the pillow and with difficulty developing a gentle rasp at the back of her throat.

If Skim were here he would be up, standing ready, a wrench in his hand. He would protect her.

When she heard the door handle rotating (the noisy confidence a warning!) she maintained the pretence of sleep, serious in her bid to avoid danger, but screwing herself down ready to bear pain.

She had no plans for the pain. She would just scratch and scream until it ended. Saliva was running out of her open mouth. It was uncomfortable and irritating, the mucus soaking into the pillow beneath her cheek, but she dared not alter her imitation. She feared making mistakes. It was possible she wouldn't be able to move even if she wanted to. She imagined weapons: a knife in his hand, a club raised, the teeth of a meat saw resting on her neck—she'd probably do nothing, continue snoring . . .

She could place his position in the room by each sound,

however tiny, and she was shocked to hear him sit on the other bed—there came the unmistakable sound, so often heard before, of the springs squeezed by weight. She worked diligently at her complete stillness; she studied each breath, checking that the sound was even. What did he want? If he had come to steal, wouldn't he be searching in drawers? Her nose was running onto the pillow, adding to the soaking mess and discomfort. She was stuck in her own snot. Her mind ached with sustained, rational fear. She allowed an eyelid to lift, just the most minute fraction, but all she saw was the trembling of her own blurred eyelashes, and the wall. She wished that she had faced the other way, but of course she had instinctively turned away from the danger when adopting her pose. She felt suddenly like an underwater organism, so abruptly resorting to camouflage in order to avoid the predator.

Skim would already have fought for her—she could see his wrench held aloft, coming down twice, three times. She would have been saved from this.

She might drown in these liquids falling from her nose and mouth. They tickled badly. The boiling content of her bladder, barely controlled with full contraction of her interior muscles, was threatening to pierce through. She felt sick, but held it.

The sinister low honk of the bedsprings sounded. The intruder had stood up. She counted her life in seconds, and each footfall shortened the wait for violence by a third. Then there was silence. She could hear the man's breath, and the slight rustle of his clothes moving against his skin as he leaned over her, but she didn't move, she was locked into her make-believe.

At the touch of the hand on her shoulder Gabriella felt a jet of urine escape her and soak along her clothes. She got ready to be hurt. While she was building up to strike out in fury, to scream, to scratch, and then run, she heard her own name spoken gently.

175

"Gabriella . . . Gabriella."

She opened her eyes to see Skim's face a short distance away looming down through the bedroom darkness.

In the same rush she felt love and shame. She threw her arms around Skim's neck and shouted his name as though he had saved her but then she shoved him off because she realized that her cheek, her lips, her chin, were sopping. She knew there would be a rank smell waiting to escape. "I must go," she said, getting out of bed and pressing the bedclothes down. "I must go to the loo." She ran from the room.

Skim went and sat on his own bed. He was relieved to be back, and this was a nice surprise. He knew that she liked him, but even so, she had almost hurt his neck with that clench—and the speed of her reaction! Skim felt that fresh ground had been put under his feet. The gap between him and the rest of the human race had narrowed. He sat on his own bed, and felt utterly careless.

"Fuck Julia!" he thought to himself.

Gabriella returned. Skim smelled the new application of perfume. She was wearing less: only the T-shirt (long enough). He watched the whites of her thighs twinkling across the room. She didn't get back into bed, she just sat down, with her knees closed, propped against each other. This added to the sum of evidence.

"Why are you here?" asked Gabriella. "I thought you are going away."

"Missed the train," said Skim, and he found an excuse on the tip of his tongue. He used it. "My bag was stolen."

"Ohh . . ." she sounded sympathy. "Julia?"

"I presume she missed it too. I don't know."

He stood up and went over to Gabriella, the danger in the deed exciting him. He took her upturned face in his hands. The whites of her eyes gleamed, the pupils were lost in the dark, colorless and empty and surmounted by heavy, drawn-down eyebrows. She looked miserable. He lowered

176

his mouth to hers, losing eye contact, but her lips, although they stayed there, didn't move to allow him in. He pulled back, and after looking at the distress in her face, he started toward seating himself next to her, on her bed. It was *Julia* making him do this.

Gabriella pushed at him then got up abruptly and took his hand, dragging him off across the room to his bed. She seemed to be moving from one emergency to another.

They had moved into a sexual arena. Speech would be tricky. They waited.

Skim wondered what had caused her reluctance, and the sudden move. He thought, "She's sensitive about using Marek's bed." He enjoyed the recklessness.

Gabriella got up, dragged all the blankets and sheets and pillows from her bed and in a frenzy gathered them all up in her arms like she needed enough to cope with a giant shock. Then she waded next door to Molly's empty room.

Skim all at once felt responsibility returning. There was pain in their actions. He could hear her organizing in there. Should he follow her?

He slid the tape machine out from under his pillow, mounted the earphones on his head, and pressed the Play button. He felt mangled, and low enough to recognize that there came a point where you got so low that you just dropped and fell. He was waiting for that to happen, but he was determined that this must be the worst, this point he'd reached, where he could see how low was possible. The music vibrated through him, stirring his thoughts toward his friends, the people that were around him. He had stumbled into this degree of intensity. He hadn't seen it coming, but wasn't this what he'd always wanted? He remembered all those evenings lying back and having his brain burn with abstract thoughts—how unpopulated by people his personal landscape had been then. Unconnected, idling in neutral, he had rambled from work to home and back to work.

He wondered again whether or not he should go next-door and apologize to Gabriella.

Perhaps not; it felt right lying on his back in bed. He'd been floored and damaged by Julia—and it was exactly this hurt that had made him go for Gabriella. He'd been greedy for any sign of affection. He had moved on her because she was vulnerable. They were in the same boat. They ought to stick together?

He lifted his bedclothes and moved heavily out into the hallway. The floor shook under his weight. There was no reply when he tapped on her door, but he went in anyway. The mound of Molly's possessions appeared in a dim silhouette against the light coming in from the street through the front windows, and somewhere in the shadows, in the foothills of Molly's pile, lay Gabriella in the improvised bed that she had made. Skim nosed forward, calling her name.

He found her with her face buried in a pillow. He couldn't persuade her to talk. He put a hand on her shoulder and gave it a series of gentle tugs. She refused to turn. When he noticed that she was shaking under his hand he felt a sudden slide of remorse. He pulled hard, hauling at her shoulder—he had to turn her round. He wanted her to see his sympathy. "Come on," he said, commanding her, and increasing the pull on her shoulder. She finally gave up when resistance seemed ridiculous, giving a moan of disappointment. When he saw her face he was shocked. Her expression had crumpled. Everything seemed to be in the wrong place. Her mouth was moving involuntarily, in spite of her, like a display of emotional spasticity. Her eyes were bogged down in their sockets, wet, pleading with him to let her go. Skim felt something inside running at him, and he ducked his face into the pillow beside her, partly to prevent her from seeing what was going to show on his face—and to avoid having to look at her.

178

He pressed her head closer to his, and felt her hand come to rest very lightly on his ribs.

His breath was heating the pillow.

He changed from holding her head to stroking it. His thumb caught her eyelash, which was wet and jerking like a bird's wing. He moved his thumb back and chased the tear down the side of her temple, smearing it into her hair. He repeated the action several times, and he felt her arm move round his back to enclose him.

As she squeezed him closer to her, Gabriella gasped—it was as if she had finally found the one large sob that had inexplicably gone missing, the one that she had been unable to find when she had cried earlier in Santay's room. The involuntary exhalation of air led her into an abrupt panic, but when she felt Skim at first breathe heavily, and then start up himself in sympathy, she felt a blessing descend. It was acceptance. It was OK. Her own crying began to spin out more freely. They shook together like they were on a bumpy car ride. Their hands moved.

When she next looked down along the length of her body she saw her own breasts pointing at Skim's chest, and the bottom half of his torso bunched and aiming into her. Marek. His name was painted like a sign in her head. And pregnancy. Her muscles tightened; Skim's breath came faster and he began surfing her in an altogether different manner. His face looked masked off, miles away. Why wasn't he looking at her? She lifted her legs so that she could get a heel in behind his knee. She put more effort into it because he was beginning to grunt. She pushed him off with her legs and hands—through the one hand on his throat she sensed the passing vibration as a strange noise of complaint came to his lips. When she felt the thread of semen leap across her stomach she went into a spasm of kicking and pushing and screaming that had him off her, away from her and standing like a dumb man by the door.

179

Gabriella, breathing heavily from the exertion, couldn't recognize herself in this situation. She turned on her elbow and dived into the pillow. She wished with all her heart that he would go away.

Skim called her name. She refused him any reply.

He begged her.

Nothing. He turned away.

His penis pointed like an anterior rudder as he followed it through the hallway back to his own room. Without the light from the street outside it was much darker in here. Annoying floor-dwelling objects spiked his fumbling walk.

He stood naked, leaning over the table, looking down at his body: the meaty stinking feet; the hairy legs, comprising large mechanical knees and oversized thighs; the hidden intricacies of all the vulgar organs arranged so haphazardly inside his torso; the sprung curliness of his hair; his fleshy face; the blood singing inside his head; the incomprehensible electrical circuitry that was fusing these thoughts *now*; and there, the fat, gleaming, magic wand that swung in front of him. He wanted to cut it off. The internal, the most important part of him, was cowering from all this fleshiness. It was huddled in the corner, frightened by his body's grossness.

"It is in there . . ." remembered Skim, "but it wants to get out."

He closed his eyes and imagined escaping from himself. He lifted out of his own body; he could picture himself below, with his arms sticking out, resting on the table. He continued traveling away.

GABRIELLA FLINCHED, TUGGING the covers over her head . . . She'd heard him use his own door handle. Then there came the sound of a fast, heavy trot up the stairs. A door opening and closing. More footsteps on the staircase—higher up. The house shook. A different door

180

slammed. She listened avidly as the noises became more distant—but maybe they were staying still, and it was she who was falling. She begged for answers. Finally, she heard a faint cry far above her.

CHRISTMAS DAY HAD arrived, it was unavoidable, swinging in like an iron ball on a chain.

THIRTY-FIVE

⏀

IT WAS GHOSTLY quiet. The offices stood empty. The streets were clean of the humming cars. There were no people.

Santay was awake (of course), and on this festival morning he felt even more than usual like a child without presents. The distant hysterical whoop of a car alarm ran unchecked, a fast loop of sound. His bedside radio had by now become an intelligent and interesting friend. He listened to Christmas cheer beamed in on invisible waves, and dribbled the last of the paraffin into the two stoves.

Later in the morning Gabriella came to find him. They exchanged Christmas presents. She'd given him a cross between a piece of jewelry and a badge, a skull-and-cross-bones design with the words I COULD EAT A HORSE written underneath in large wobbly capital letters. He pinned it on immediately.

He had given her a collection of small presents which he'd put in a long red sock.

"This is clean this sock?" asked Gabriella, swinging it in front of him.

"Of course."

"I'm no so sure. You dreadful with your socks. Often I see them lying on the floor for weeks."

"They wash themselves. They go up to the first-floor bathroom. You can see them leaning over the sink, sometimes."

She took her time with the unwrapping, exclaiming with each present.

"What was that racket?" asked Santay. "I heard bumps and crashes, and then voices . . ."

Gabriella found herself nearly having to tell lies again, it was so close to that, not telling the whole truth.

"Skim," she said, nonchalantly. "He had to break in. His bag was stolen. He missed his train . . ."

"I was scared stiff for a while. You ought to have seen me. My arms out, maximum stretch, the barrel of the pistol aiming at the door, for God's sake, and then the relief, hearing you talking!"

"The pistol is not still here?"

"No, no. It should have been. I'd have needed it last night."

Gabriella veered off the topic, into the motions of Christmas. They were going to attempt an oddball fried version of Christmas dinner, using the camping stove.

They'd found themselves clear of any dangerous topics, going along all right, when Mrs. Gorse unlocked the front door and effortfully came in. She called out their names, and Gabriella went to meet her in the hallway. They came back down to Santay's room, followed by a student carrying a straw shopping bag.

"Gabriella and Santay, Happy Christmas." She was smiling hugely with this, she had no festive embarrassment. She turned to her student and waved a hand, trying to think of his name. She failed, but carried on, turning back to Santay and Gabriella.

"How are you? How is my house? You know, I forget what it is like, dear dear house! It makes me, oh"—she rested a hand on her chest—"I don't know, alive again, to be in my house. Now! Christmas! So I have brought presents."

Gabriella and Santay exclaimed their surprise.

". . . Nonsense, poor things, alone, at Christmas! Here!" She shoved the box on Santay's lap.

"Here!"

She waved a plastic bag at Gabriella while still looking into the depths of the basket. Gabriella had to grab her present as it moved. She looked like a kitten, catching it.

"A plug . . . where is the plug?" she asked the unfortunate student, who shrugged and made a tentative move toward the basket.

Mrs. Gorse pointed at the box which Santay was unwrapping.

"That's electric," she said, "it needs a plug." She stared at the box impatiently, and he speeded up his unwrapping. "A white shoe box," said Santay. He took the lid off to reveal the second-hand telephone. Mrs. Gorse checked his face.

"The last thing," she wagged a finger. "D'you remember when we got this"—she pointed at the bar hanging over the bed—"and this"—she pointed to the computer—"and this!"—the television. "I told you we'd get one of these for you, didn't I tell you? Happy Christmas!" She leaned forward, tears forced to jump out from the blink of her eyes. They joined cheeks and kissed the air. "And the plug, the plug!" exclaimed Mrs. Gorse, turning to her basket again.

She fished out a three-pin electrical plug and handed it to him.

Santay took it politely. She was offering him this giant thirteen-amp fused plug for the phone? He thought what an odd world it must be inside Mrs. Gorse's head; for her everything traveled down the same wires, whether it was electricity, radio waves, or telephone conversations. They

184

were all jumbled up together and came out through the bottom of the wall.

"Chairs, chairs," said Mrs. Gorse to the student, who started guiltily and meandered into a search round the room.

"I've already got one," said Santay.

"Yes," said Mrs. Gorse, tapping his arm and cackling merrily like a Mother Christmas in a pantomime, "soon me too!" She dumped herself into the chair that the student had brought from the corner. Gabriella sat on the bed. The student stood, awkwardly, folding his arms.

"Now tell me, what's been happening in my house?"

Gabriella and Santay looked at each other. "Nothing much," said Gabriella lightly.

"Parties," said Mrs. Gorse, "loud poppy music, naked bodies all over the place? Watch out I don't cut your balls off," she said to Santay.

"You may as well," he replied, but she didn't hear because she was laughing at her own rudeness. She swayed an inch or two back and forth in her chair.

"There's no one else here?" she asked. "All gone back to their mummies for Christmas?"

"Skim's here," said Gabriella, "he miss his train so his here by mistake."

"Where?" asked Mrs. Gorse.

Gabriella hadn't seen him that morning, she hadn't wanted to go and meet the findings of their new intimacy. They should keep away from each other, she felt: to each one their own loss.

"I think his in his room. I don' know, he hasn't appeared yet."

"Oh my God," said Mrs. Gorse in mock urgency, "I haven't got him a present. Oh no dear God."

She leaned over (it was difficult, she didn't seem to be flexible at the middle) and with the very tips of her two fingers caught up the bit of brown paper that Santay had

185

discarded onto the floor when he was unwrapping his telephone.

"Skim, for Skim, what does he like?" she asked no one in particular. Both Gabriella and Santay were nonplussed at her urgency. She peered around her for the straw basket, found it, and jerked it up onto her lap.

"Christmas . . ." she muttered.

"Have you got a present for everyone you meet?" asked Santay. He was left listening to his own words while Mrs. Gorse fished out a tired-looking blue shirt with an old-fashioned collar from the shopping bag.

"Of course not," she replied, "only special people, good people. What do you think about this? Will he like this?"

They·could see that it was made to fit a seven-year-old child.

"Fine," they agreed.

Mrs. Gorse bound the shirt tightly in the paper from the telephone but she had no sellotape. She held the package in her hand.

"Where is he?" she asked.

Gabriella and Mrs. Gorse and the reluctant student went to Skim's room, following Gabriella's lead. Santay rolled himself to the bottom of the three stairs to watch the ceremony.

Gabriella knocked and listened. There was no reply, nor even a sound of movement.

"He can't be still asleep," said Gabriella. Mrs. Gorse was looking at her as though she, Gabriella, was in control of the operation, so she opened the door, trying to ignore the discomfort. They went in.

"Hawkins!" cried Mrs. Gorse.

Hawkins looked up balefully from the hole he had made in the swirl of blankets on Skim's bed.

"Oh my Hawkins!" said Mrs. Gorse again, stepping toward him.

An astute look came into Hawkins's face, and he unfolded one paw in front of him, ready.

Mrs. Gorse lunged, but he was gone, through the slalom course of people's legs in a trice. The room was empty.

"He came home," said Mrs. Gorse. "Gabriella, you must feed him. Until we get back, will you feed him?"

Gabriella agreed.

"Skim must have gone out," she added.

"Without saying Happy Christmas?" Mrs. Gorse was incredulous. She remembered the present in her hand. After looking at it for a while she put it back in the shopping bag.

"When he returns you must tell him that no one deserves a present if they treat Christmas just like it is a day off. No one behaves like that in Chapel Street. No one. Not even him. Tell him from me."

She was beginning to negotiate the tunnel through the piled-up walls of paraphernalia, but she turned round, treading the stair carpet to come back down to Santay.

"Happy Christmas," she said to him, with a sudden return to cheeriness. He was struck by her face bumping into his. She delivered an equal affection to Gabriella before she left.

Gabriella went into Skim's empty room again. There was absolute silence; she stood in the middle and, bit by bit, turned a full circle. Maybe he was trying to avoid what had happened. She was holding her breath.

She left quickly, and descended the three stairs.

Santay was waiting in his doorway. "He must have found someone to go and see. What did he have planned?"

He reversed into his room, clearing a path for her. He was now stationed over by the window, next to the large cold squares of grimy glass.

"I don' know," she replied. "He has no got any keys."

She became reluctant to talk. Where was Skim?

Santay stayed by the window while Gabriella tried on the

headscarf that Mrs. Gorse had given her. It had a picture of a horse on it—Gabriella had once said that she'd ridden a horse before. She looked ludicrous.

"Too much has happened," said Gabriella. "Stop, everything stop. I want to go backward."

She ducked to avoid the bar and rolled onto Santay's bed.

"It's a strange Christmas," said Santay.

"Yes. Stranger. The strangest. I will never forget it."

Santay smeared the window to look out, trying to dodge the opacity of condensation and dirt.

"So far away from home," said Gabriella. "I have never been away at Christmas. Is an empty day . . . funny. Is completely empty, there's nothing in today."

Santay was peering over to Skim and Marek's window. "I wonder where he's got to?"

Gabriella lolled slowly toward the door. "I'll look around," she said.

She trekked up to the first floor. Nothing. The rooms stood at ease, stately, unused. She continued upward, her footsteps sounding hollowly.

The second floor offered nothing. Nor the third.

It was strange to go up to the attic. She hadn't been up here for a while. It smelt spicy with dust.

The window in the kitchenette was pushed wide open. "Oh no . . ." groaned Gabriella, and leaned out to have a look. But she could see no sign of him.

After leaning on the sill for some while she returned downstairs, trotting, dizzy by the time she reached the bottom.

"The window's open up in the attic," she told Santay.

They looked at each other, a certain casual sort of dread beginning to rise at the sudden responsibility of finding out where Skim had got to.

"I see if his car is there," she said.

"I thought it was broken down," replied Santay.

"I don' know . . ." she said, her words trailing as she left, heading toward the outside. Santay waited at the foot of the three stairs. Gabriella had left the front door open and he could see a portion of her from the shoulders up, moving slowly toward the other side of the street. She was looking up and down the length of the road, scouting for Skim's car. She turned round when she got to the other side, and faced the house, looking up. She stopped then, her head angled backward, staring, with her mouth open. She moved both hands to cup her mouth.

"Skim!"

She dropped her hands.

Santay was impatient for information, and called, "Gabriella!" The shout seemed too loud for indoors. He got no reply.

"Skim!" Gabriella repeated her shout, and waited.

Then again she lifted her hands to funnel the sound more effectively. He saw her draw the breath, but she decided not to call.

He watched her as she came back toward him, leaving the front door still open behind her. She sat on the top stair, perplexed.

"His up there," she said, "sitting between two chimneys."

Santay laughed in disbelief. "What? What's he doing?"

"I don' know. When I call he was facing the other way, and he turns"—her hand described the motion—"but he did no say anything. He look down at me, and I think he was smiling. He did no look unhappy, or anything. But he didn' wave. He did no say one word. He looks down, and as though he didn' know who I was."

"What was he wearing?"

"Normal clothes. Coat. Everything."

They both felt that the ground had shifted. The puzzle was giving them a slight pleasure, as well as concern.

"What's he up to? D'you know any reason why?" asked Santay.

"No . . ."

Gabriella got to her feet and went into his room. It refused to give her any clues. Was it her fault?

She went up to the attic and climbed out of the kitchenette window, gesticulating, scooping the air to try and signal him down. No result.

Gabriella and Santay waited for the whole afternoon, discussing the problem and trying to resolve their responsibilities. They both pretended to be experienced in emergency; they had one or two stories each, about friends of friends.

When the sooty darkness closed and Skim was still up there, Gabriella (she felt self-conscious, like an old lady with a cat stuck in a tree) called the police. Christmas Day ended for them with the glittering, noisy spectacle of a bright red crane working under the headlights of police vehicles, all emergency lights swinging. They looked like expensive full-size toys.

Skim observed from above, unmoved by any advice given to him through the loud hailer, half of him in shadow, half of him brightly lit, like the moon.

THIRTY-SIX

THE NEW YEAR was approaching—the mechanism of the grandmother clock would blithely mark it. Its tocking and gonging was at that time the only noise in the house: deep, hollow, wooden. It kept going in its new position, measuring, measuring—but even if it were to stop, no matter, Time had a clockwork line of years marching overhead, each one with a twelve-month stride.

The phone summoned them shrilly.

Santay rolled himself from Molly's room into the hallway. He prodded the receiver off the hook and caught it.

"Hello?"

He listened. Silence. Heavy breathing. Then came Mrs. Gorse's voice: "Who's that?"

"Santay."

"Santay, Santay oh my God."

"What's up?"

"Where am I?" demanded Mrs. Gorse.

Santay was puzzled; he waited because he thought it was a rhetorical question. Her voice came again, sounding hurt: "I don't know where I am!"

"You don't know?" queried Santay. Gabriella had

joined him, she leaned against the wall and interleaved her arms. Santay tried again: "What happened?"

"I've forgotten." She sounded angry.

"Mrs. Gorse, stay calm. Where are you calling from? Is it a public phone box?"

"I don't know. Box? What box?"

"Look about you. Where are you?"

"I'm in a room. A strange room. Brown. There is a pile of books . . . my books!"

"Read the telephone dial. What does the telephone dial say?" Santay was looking at Gabriella, who mouthed a silent question. A look of mystery settled on her face.

"Six two," began Mrs. Gorse. There was a pause. She breathed, sucked the roof of her mouth, and started again: "Six two two, three six seven oh."

Santay repeated the number; Gabriella watched his mouth, following it for herself. She stopped halfway on the second time through. "Is her home number," she whispered indignantly. "Thass her new home number, tell her."

"Mrs. Gorse, that's your new home number. You're in your new flat. Hello?"

Someone had interrupted her. Miniature, hollow sounds of a struggle came down the line. Mrs. Gorse was being ticked off! A fresh voice hijacked the receiver.

"Hello?" enquired Santay.

"Hello, it's Greta here, Mrs. Gorse's daughter. Who am I speaking to?"

"It's Santay."

"Hello Santay. I'm sorry."

"What's happening?"

"It's a long story. I've come to stay for a bit; Mumma . . . well, she needs a bit of help at the moment. It's chaotic over here. While I've got you on the line . . ."

"Yes?"

"How many of you are actually there?"

"Two of us. Me, Gabriella. Marek comes back tomorrow.

192

Skim, er, is . . ."—he decided not to say anything—"isn't here at the moment, and there's Julia . . . quite a few, why?"

"It's a very sad thing . . ."

"What?"

"The surveyor's letter came today. The report."

"What report?"

"About the timbers. He says that the house is completely rotten. Everything must be pulled out."

"For definite?"

"Yes definite."

Suddenly he was listening to a skirmish. Mrs. Gorse came back on the line, cutting through the impatient moan of complaint from her daughter. "Is Skim there?" she asked.

"No, he's not."

Santay released the receiver a fraction—he had been pressing it too hard up against his ear. Gabriella was watching him carefully.

There was a muffled conversation on the other end. Greta won the telephone back from Mrs. Gorse.

"Hello?"

"Hello."

"Sorry, yes, it's gone beyond the electricity now, I'm afraid. Is the workman still there?"

The objects that belonged to the electrician—the overalls collapsed lifeless over the bottom of the banister, the tools, the working boots, and the yellow plastic snake that carried empty bulb-holders up the stairs—all these things had vanished.

"No, it doesn't look like it."

"It's not just the wiring. The house has got rot, according to the survey. There aren't that many years left on our lease, and I think it might be a case of accepting the freeholder's offer."

"What offer?"

"He wants to buy out our remaining lease. He's going to refurbish."

"Agh."

"I know. There's nothing I can do. I have to go ahead, really, with Mumma like this at the moment . . ."

"What's happened?"

"I . . . Are you there next week?"

"Yes."

"I'll call then. Can I leave it for now? I'm sure you can appreciate . . ."

"All right, yes, all right. But tell me, this means we have to move out completely?"

There was a pause. "Yes."

"Bugger," said Santay. He felt a slow dreariness spread like a stain inside him.

"I'm sorry." The apology came crackling down the line.

Santay suffered a virulent hatred as he put the phone down. To think of the microscopic jaws of a fungus slowly eating away all around him! He'd be well out of all this.

Gabriella looked as glum as he did. They discussed the consequences for a short while, then he asked her to take him back down to his room. He wanted to deal with the bad news alone.

To be forced to move out of here—his room for so many years! He swore. There was a conspiracy against him. He screwed his neck round to see out of the window. The clouds were flat-bottomed and they gathered in formation like freshly built ships, absurdly shaped, massive, sailing in a gray sky, shot through with mock structural rods of sunlight.

Sailing against him?

He tilted his head back to its natural position. His more usual enemies still stood at the back of his mind like fairground skittles, impossible to knock down: Insomnia, Pity, Neediness.

GABRIELLA HAD A fit of cleaning the next day. She felt anxious about the amount of grit in the house. It crunched like sugar when you stepped on the bare boards. The rugs, tough old things, were failing to absorb it any more. They were full up. She clattered fiercely on the stairs with a dustpan and broom: the dust swam the air all day.

She longed for her attic room to retreat to for a while. "To find my true self . . ." No matter that it was so small. She had no sooner been given it than it had been taken away. She thought, "I need it now, I want to retreat."

Marek was coming home.

She was insecure. There was deep water beneath her feet; she couldn't easily keep upright. She longed to escape the ordinariness of her situation. It was without glamor. "Reality," she murmured to herself as she gave the next stair downward a stiff raking with the broom. Then she added a question mark, and then took it away again. "Real love," she thought, three stairs down, "how hilarious."

Marek was getting nearer. The place was a mess. She cleaned and cleaned. Still it was a mess.

She had a New Year's resolution: "I will not tell a lie again." Yet she could feel this big one rising, and wouldn't it save her, wouldn't it let everyone off a nasty time? No, she knew it was the opposite with lies. They were cancerous things—this one might be enough to take her and everyone else with it.

Later she was pacing up and down Molly's room, in front of Molly's possessions. Perhaps she should lift the sheet, walk under there, and let it drop back, shroud herself, remain motionless among the other boxes and look like a resting lamp stand. Marek would walk in . . .

There were other things she could tell him, great gobs of clean truth: the wood rot, and Skim in hospital.

Marek would be humming his way to the house.

Play it by ear? Play it straight.

She sat against the wall, legs flat on the floor in front of her because there was a fresh crease in her trousers (for him). She told herself to relax. If a lie came out, it came out.

It would save her, but then it would turn and eat her up. The truth, though, would guzzle her for a start, then Marek, the main course. Skim for afters. Did she want to be eaten now or later?

"I give up from myself," she murmured. Oh yes, there it was again, the usual attempt at abdication. She looked at the tips of her toes. Her legs were laid out like two logs. "I can't be responsible for all this," she thought.

Marek was ready to engage in their reunion to the full extent. He felt quite new, seeing her again.

Gabriella greeted him with difficulty. The sight of him suddenly appearing in the doorway made her feel wrong. She had a secret from him.

He approached happily, ambling toward her with his arms open, ready to squeeze her.

She stepped backward and gently knocked aside his usual hold of her, preventing him, anxious to be different in some way from how they'd been before. She wanted to keep her groin away from his. Grief! Most especially she grieved that he didn't know. She felt a vulgar urge to confess.

"Marek . . ."

"What? What is it?"

"Skim," began Gabriella, feeling the lie near.

Marek's eyebrows rose. "Skim? What about Skim?"

"He had a . . ." (what was it?) ". . . a flip," she said, "he wen' up to the roof and refuse to come down. They come and took him. He says nothing, nobody knows nothing."

"What? A flip? What happened to him?"

"He didn' say. Juss tired or something. They took him into a psychiatric ward. To have a short stay. It was Christmas, they don' know what to do. His agreed."

"Have you seen him?"

"No."

"Are there no visitors?"

"Yes, I think you can visit." The lie was there like a ghost in her mouth. Marek couldn't see it, but it was there. "I did no visit," she continued, "because I thought he wan' to get away from us, from the house and everything."

Marek looked like an actor left deserted on the stage. His face, grimy from train travel, dropped in surprise. He stood at a civilized distance from her, his arms folded: in a hug of himself. He queued with quiet rows of questions. When? How? Why didn't she ring? He would have come straight back. This was more than enough to explain her changed mood.

Still they hadn't touched. He wanted to stroke her, but he was afraid, and also confused. Why had she jilted him? That initial step backward; the slight push with her wrist; it was enough: the first rejection from someone who had always wanted to be wound in his arms. He'd returned a stranger to the thread of her life. It made him determined never to leave her again for as long as one single day.

After they'd finished talking Gabriella held him gently, carefully, against her, with a delicacy that was more erotic than she'd previously known with him before.

Her guilt, too, was sensual, it pinned her down under him—a mental trap.

MAREK SET OUT to see Skim that afternoon. His hair, longer than before, swung in a counter-motion to the tilt of his metronomic walk. He got on the bus and began the new journey.

Marek invented notions of what a psychiatric ward would have done to his friend. He was ready for tragedy: Skim would be a vegetable, or mentally wild. There would be drugs in his blood. Perhaps he wouldn't be able to talk.

He tried to remember any hint that might have warned him of this. There was nothing. Skim was an ordinary man, as ordinary as this bus journey, as those trees sliding past, sane as this woman sitting next to him . . . Marek's eye was held by the violently colored label in the woman's shopping basket. "Bonky." He scrutinized the jar, ascertaining that it was the trade name for a foreign hot chocolate drink. "*Bonky?*" he asked himself. "Is that really normal?" He glanced secretly at the stern face of the woman herself. What maddening regrets did she have? The bus was a miracle of ingenuity, what with the barely harnessed anarchy of its physics, the thousands of explosions constantly under the bonnet, but bolted down, restrained. The trees were making a crazy effort to suck water and breathe light for no good reason. The kids were wild with their skates and their bicycles, thoughtless in their mad pattern of fun.

"The earth will open and swallow us all up," thought Marek, imagining the center of the earth being revealed to him, a vast muddy heart pumping greedily. Was the earth an animal?

Marek formulated a plan (for use in his visit) to treat madness as if it was always there, in him, in everyone, in the trees and the children and the bus engine. It was the normal state, but strict controls prevented it from causing trouble. Like the bolts for the engine. Skim had been undone—"a screw loose" (Marek suddenly, with satisfaction, arrived at the English expression).

He started on a score for this opera of horror, with the bus engine a constant roar, the tinkling conversation of old ladies talking over one another, and the arrhythmical clumping steps of passengers caught off-balance on the stairs.

He was feeling anxious; the soles of his feet were itching.

The bus ride took him farther from the places he knew and into a desert of cheap buildings and massed population.

He fell to thinking about Gabriella. It had always been like an affectionate gossiping with himself within a set, fenced-off area of his mind, but now it was an uncomfort-

198

able place to be, this special reserve of thought dedicated to the preservation of his love for her.

Because, he thought, absently focusing on the details of the neck of the traveler in front of him, he had to admit that she was looking at him in a different way.

What was it that had slipped? Did she no longer love him? Shouldn't all this make her more needy of him?

Marek was tempted to return to her immediately, but Skim's predicament stopped the impulse. What a mess. His heart ached for his friend, and for himself. He curled his toes to try and relieve the irritation hidden in the arches of his feet.

When he got off the bus he bought a bag of chocolate Brazils. He meandered for a while, consulting the map, growing more certain of his direction.

Blue nylon-covered chairs and orange paint greeted him when he arrived. This was a psychiatric ward. It was enough to drive you mad. Swinging doors and locks; everything screwed down.

He pursued his enquiry with various staff until he fetched up in a waiting room, not alone but with others, all silent and careful with the fall of their glances. He was summoned, and he followed the square hips of a nurse until the view was unblocked and he could see that he was in a large room. Skim's ward.

Skim was sitting among others at the far end of the room. When Marek saw him rise and start walking in his direction he knew that his friend was all right. The big body filled the room as before! He smiled and waved, and walked quickly to meet him halfway.

As he watched, Skim smacked face-first into a concrete pillar in the middle of the room.

There had been an old lady, her body curled forward, half-hitching herself across the room in another direction. Skim had hopped in front of her and turned to glance back as she went behind him, looking forward again just in time to smash his face into the colonette standing in his path. He'd bounced backward and the old lady, in her turn, ricocheted off his hip as though she'd been struck by a moving car. She fell over sideways. She didn't even have time to put an arm out to save herself. Bang.

There was a confusion. She lay like a damaged insect, pathetically moving. She'd bumped her head—nurses came running and surrounded her. Out of the mess came Skim, still walking toward Marek. He was behaving as though nothing had happened.

Marek touched his own forehead and nose, in sympathy with Skim's blows. He was nervous and unsure of his position. He studied Skim's face for a reaction. He had been frightened by the incident, and he wanted to help the old lady, but Skim had taken control and was leading him by the arm back to the chairs. One of the nurses who was helping the old lady to her feet gave them both a black look. Marek felt implicated: they were a couple of yobs.

They went and sat down, Skim still holding Marek's hand.

"Marek, Marek!" he exclaimed. He was smiling. It was a sight, him looking so happy. "How are you?" he asked.

"I'm all right," said Marek, startled, and then, expecting this question to signal the beginning of a long explanation, "How are you?"

"I am exactly as you see me," said Skim mysteriously, "a simple fucking Joe Bloggs bloke. But . . ."

"What?"

Skim was wagging his head from side to side and skinning his eyeballs in a series of brief stares. He'd been watching too much breakfast television. The little graphic device, the clock in the bottom right-hand corner, had imprinted itself; he couldn't shake it off. It was the only part of the program he'd looked at.

"What?"

Skim took Marek's other hand as well. He studied Marek's face and then said, "I'm sorry about Gabriella."

"How d'you mean?"

"Know what?" asked Skim. "I think it's possible that wrong, that wrongness doesn't exist. Morality? You see I never had it yet I've suddenly really got it, understood it. Morality is a fucking set of rules, but . . . it doesn't matter what the rules are, not really. And people hardly ever commit wrong. They nearly always do what they think is right at the time. After all if they want to do it, it must feel right, mustn't it? How about that? Everybody is right, blowing up a plane, or sleeping with your best friend's girl, everybody's doing what they think is right. It's just that none of it coincides, so it's all pain. There's pain, fucking reams of the stuff, endless pain, but no actual wrong. What d'you think?"

"I'm not sure," said Marek. "How does being sorry about Gabriella come into it?"

"Your truly good person is the one who understands others' pain, I think, and doesn't cause it. And not living in your own pain, on purpose sometimes, some people do. But me and Gabriella. I was a different person then." Skim squeezed Marek's hand. "You've got to believe me," he urged, "please! I was wrecked. And then . . ." He stopped.

"I don't understand," said Marek. He had never seen Skim like this. Talking so much, so fast!

Opposite them a middle-aged woman was beating herself on the side of her head with a fist. Others were watching to see what would happen.

"I'm not really meant to be here," continued Skim. "They didn't count me as mad. It was Christmas, they had nowhere else to put me. I got over-excited. Fuck for good reason though. I needed a rest, I just needed a rest."

Marek couldn't get over the alteration. It was as though an enthusiastic amateur actor had invaded his friend.

Happiness on that particular face looked bizarre. He wanted to talk to a doctor or someone in charge, but there were only nurses, and they were going too fast to ask.

Instead there was the handover of the chocolate Brazils.

"I don't deserve you," said Skim, and then after a while he continued, "at least I do now, didn't then. Just at the last minute. What a thing to happen. It was me, my fault. I'm sorry." Skim steadily popped the chocolate nuts.

"Why did you go up to the chimneys?" asked Marek.

"In one word?" Skim was chewing hard. "God!" Then he shook his head again, angry at himself, as though this had been a mistake. "No, not God. Not that old fool but what God is, the vision behind the puppet, what the name really is, what everyone else . . ." He paused, waiting for his argument to become clear to him. "I have discovered," he said, very deliberately picking his way through, "the truth behind all those bloody stories." This lucid statement calmed him, and he stopped there for a while, his jaws coming to rest as he nodded, reinforming himself of the discovery.

Then he turned to Marek, and he had eyes as wet as oysters. "I'm sorry," he muttered, "you can have my biggest fucking sorry, please!" He dragged Marek under his wing, into a hug. "If I could undo it I would have no problem with doing just fucking that, really, really . . ."

Marek had to move apart from the embrace to hear what Skim was saying. Why did he keep shaking his head?

"That's almost *why* it happened," continued Skim.

"What?"

"Because of Gabriella!"

Marek didn't understand but he pretended to. He nodded. Skim, seeing his friend's moustache twitch and his eyes glaze with worried incomprehension, gave his new smile and said, "Don't worry. I'll explain, I'll explain it all." Then he smiled again. It looked fixed, or painted on.

He lobbed another chocolate nut, and offered one to Marek.

MAREK RELATED THE details of his visit as he and Gabriella were sitting facing each other in the front room, each wrapped in a separate sleeping bag. They looked like young people camping outdoors. "It was . . . I don't know, incredible," said Marek.

The slope of his shoulders seemed to have increased. Because he himself had had a shock, he now thought he understood why Gabriella had pushed his arm away. She had needed a blanket, not a clumsy embrace. On the return journey he had become determined to remain at a certain distance from her. Not too far away—close enough to be useful.

"What happened?" she asked.

"He was talking about you, saying sorry all the time, as though you had caused it . . ." said Marek.

If Gabriella looked at herself sideways she could see there was a marginal satisfaction at being the cause of Skim's climb to the roof.

Marek watched her, with the beginnings of an accusation.

"He said that several times. It was because of you. You hadn't done it, it had to have happened, but you caused it by mistake."

"What? Cause what?"

"I don't know exactly. This discovery. The last thing he did was make me promise not to tell Julia. He wants to tell her himself. He said the odd thing about it was that it was a way out of whatever problems there are between them."

Gabriella and Marek sat facing each other, digesting the news.

"So what happened with you and Skim?" asked Marek.

203

"We 'ave a bit of a row," admitted Gabriella.

She asked then, "When's he come back?"

"According to him, next week."

"What if they say different?"

Marek shrugged. He felt hungry, but he had no money left.

They started talking about other things. They detailed themselves to odd tasks: taking the turbo containers to fetch paraffin; phone calls to Mrs. Gorse and others; buying a newspaper, more matches, and food. Gabriella's nerves settled.

She liked this—how it was now, when they spoke in low tones, a shorthand mumbling, barely louder than thoughts. It might be entirely different next week, but for now she should just enjoy—and it was pleasurable, this surging of a new type of love for Marek.

She thought, "That's what it is, he is dear to me." There he was, staring at the rug. She wanted to be equally dear to him. She willed him to look up at her, but he didn't respond. He was upset over his friend, he was being a bit distant because of that. She wished goodness on him.

THIRTY-SEVEN

❧

Mrs. Gorse appeared wrapped in an overcoat underneath which she was wearing a flowered dress. She was accompanied by her daughter Greta and several students, and a three-ton box van was parked in the street outside.

"Oh my friend," she said as she clambered up the front steps. "My house was my friend, my good friend!" She gave the front door a thump as she walked through. "This is something that today's young people don't understand." She squeezed in among her boxes, scattering plans and exclaiming.

Greta was in charge. She press-ganged Marek into helping, and handed provisions to Santay and asked him to set up a tea-and-sandwich station round the camping stove in his room. Mrs. Gorse proved to be an obstruction, so she was parked (with one student to attend her) in Santay's room.

Shouts rang through the house; the bare boards thumped with furniture. Teams formed like ants round the larger pieces.

"Everyone, we must all help each other," said Mrs.

Gorse, making her way over to a chair. Santay stacked the sliced bread.

"Yes," agreed the student trailing her.

"Who are you?" asked Mrs. Gorse.

The student looked confused. "I am your lodger."

"Don't use that word. 'Lodger'—it is like some job. You are my guest, and you give me a contribution. Give, freely. Can you drive?"

"I drove you here," replied the student. Mrs. Gorse stared in disbelief. She turned to Santay. Her face split as if an axe had fallen across it. "Oh my God," she roared in mirth, "my memory!" She rocked back and forth. "I can't remember the . . . what was it Greta said? The short term. I can't remember the short term!" She tapped her knee with her fist and pointed a finger at the student. "Mind you, there is no need to be sarcastic. If you have time there is some redecoration. I need some painting done. I don't like brown. D'you have time? This week?"

"Well . . ." began the student.

"Never mind. Sometime."

Mrs. Gorse leaned forward to check the progress of some object being carried out of the front door. She muttered under her breath.

The house was emptying fast. The pavement outside was littered with stuff. The back of the van stood open obediently, waiting for Greta's decisions. The hall was a spacious place now, several people could mill about together. The wallpaper behind where the boxes and bags had previously stood was revealed, shy and virginal; there was an outline marked in dirt and a shadow permanently etched where the light had never got to wear down the colors.

Mrs. Gorse caught sight of the student. She asked again, "Who are you?"

"You just . . . I'm . . . I'm your *guest*."

"My guest?"

"Yes, that's what you said I was."

"But you are not a friend of mine, so how can you be my guest? Do you pay, do you pay money?"

"Yes."

"Then you are a tenant, not a guest."

"You just said I was a guest," replied the student.

"Oh did I? A-ha! Ha ha ha!"

Santay wanted to record her laugh and sell it in one of those little novelty bags. "The Laughing Landlady."

OVER THE NEXT few days most of the others arrived. Molly and Claude first (they'd found a flat together). Claude was annoyed to find Julia ensconced in his room, but he tried not to show it, giving in to an elaborate display of courtesy with the Beatrix Potter animals—he walked them carefully across the room to get them out of his chairs.

Mr. Lightfoot came and methodically overlooked the efforts of two professional removal men. They called him "sir" and managed to remain polite throughout.

Claude came again; he had been detailed to help old Mr. Clary with his things. Mr. Clary's sister fended off traffic wardens by the car, while her brother took up a position— bent double, his rear against the wall—in the now cavernously empty hallway; he stared at the floor as though he was looking for a contact lens.

Claude trotted up and down; old Mr. Clary breathed and blinked. His life's gatherings collected gradually round his feet.

Santay heard a sound so slight it was like an echo: "Hello?"

He wheeled to his door, and saw the old man looking into a suitcase.

"Hello?" called Santay. He recognized the word he'd been using to start his attempts at meditation.

"Ah," said Mr. Clary. His voice came out as a slow whisper. "I seem. To have been here for. An awfully long time. I thought. Maybe I'd been forgotten about."

207

"No," said Santay reassuringly, talking slowly as though Mr. Clary was foreign, "no, Claude's upstairs, I can hear him. He'll be down in a moment. Not to worry. I'd bring you a cup of tea but I can't get up these three stairs."

"I don't. Suppose I could get down them," said Mr. Clary. "My foot is. Trapped. Underneath this suitcase."

Santay felt a stab of empathy. He breathed in. "Don't worry," he began. He saw Mr. Clary's head tilt upward. "He'll be down in a minute."

"All right."

"Are you sure? I can shout for Claude."

"I've lasted. This long. I'm not going to be. Defeated by a. A suitcase made of vinyl. But the young. Man. Moves so fast. I draw a breath. And he's gone."

Santay liked the sight of this old man. He felt an affinity with his inchmeal progress through life. His age seemed the very opposite of decrepit—he looked decayed, yes, but alive with spiritual potential.

Santay wanted that for himself. There was hope. He'd been learning how to relax: with tranquilizers he, too, could slow himself down to a brilliant stillness.

He thought, "Dear old man."

THIRTY-EIGHT

Skim's return: he walked in as though he had just come back from work.

Marek wondered again at the new mannerism, the small shake of Skim's head which was accompanied as before by a momentarily excessive peeling of his eyes. What was going to happen next with his friend, was he going to start shouting? He hardly dared get up—Skim might knock him over.

"The brilliant thing about my God," said Skim, "no, not about my GOD exactly, about my whatever, is there's nothing attached, nothing good or bad . . ." He wanted to carry on, but he came to a halt.

Marek, waiting, said, "What?"

"No, no," replied Skim, "I have to speak to Julia first."

"Have you seen her?"

"Is she back?" asked Skim, lightly.

"Yes, somewhere . . ."

Skim was not stoic about this. It was difficult for him to keep control. He exerted an internal muscle—the operation of the muscle showed clearly. Julia! He shook his head again and blinked.

"One thing," said Gabriella.

"What?" asked Skim. He was lying in bed with a "jumbo" pad of paper. He'd written several phrases and mottoes.

"Well, don' rely too much on Julia," said Gabriella.

Skim didn't have a clue what she was talking about. He knew that if there was one person worth his trust it would be Julia. He felt a nasty pity for Gabriella, suddenly. Her tactics were obvious. Nevertheless, considering his new responsibility as the inventor—no, not the inventor, more the discoverer—of the true answer that would end Man's malevolent, wildly creative search for a religion, he was trying to behave with more decorum. Not rely too much on Julia? He tried to turn an understanding, compassionate expression on Gabriella.

"No," he said with a tight voice, "I won't."

Gabriella saw that her warning had been ignored.

SKIM MANAGED TO fix a date with Julia. It was an appointment; a diplomatic event that she finally allowed to take place.

They went to a Pizza Palace, walking through their own reflections in the glass door.

Skim had certain things he wanted to say and these words were already lined up—he couldn't actually deal with anything else until they'd been shifted out of the way.

Julia shivered. She'd taken off her coat and a breeze had run down her neck. She put her coat back on again. Meanwhile Skim queued with his words.

As soon as the waiter had taken their order and brought drinks Skim took the first step—this was a strategy prepared long in advance; it had been planned minutely. The words sounded parrot-like: "I want to tell you a story."

Julia marked the looming closeness of his face and prepared to accept a story as something easier to deal with than a scene.

"One of the beetles," began Skim, "one of the beetles took off . . ."

Disbelief sprang in Julia's mind, and she forced herself not to laugh. What next? Might he have another fit in front of her? She had to work hard to settle her hysteria. It was too late—he had seen it. "Fuck that," he said, chasing and killing his own embarrassment. The story had dropped like a brick. The Pizza Palace setting was working against him.

"I've had enough of beetles," he continued, "I've been like a beetle, not far off anyway."

He added, urgently, "Julia, something has happened. I've got to tell you."

It was an authentic tone. Julia became interested. Maybe this was real life now. She'd always thought that nothing ever happened to her, but she might be involved in this. She watched as Skim prepared a fresh start.

Still waiting, she could smell warm pizza toppings and burned dough. Her mouth flooded, while her attention stayed pinned to Skim. She was equally hungry for what he was having such difficulty coming out with. He was poised in front of her as if about to make a statement to a court of law.

"I have found," he began. She felt the table jog against her as his heavy body fidgeted on the other side.

He started again. "It was a sort of out-of-body experience," said Skim.

"Oh . . . ?"

"That's how it began," continued Skim, "then I made this . . . this, I don't know what you would call it. A discovery. A discovery."

The waiter approached, swinging through the tables with their food. He served them and left. Opposite her Skim was organizing his knife and fork, impatient. She noticed that while she was already chewing indecently quickly, his first forkful stayed in the air. There was a perceptible blush

211

on his cheek. Julia wondered whether she ought to look like she was enjoying herself, or whether she ought to look graver. She felt bad about eating, while his messily pronged segment had been in transit for so long. It looked too large to fit in his mouth.

"So," he said, and tried a lighthearted smile.

Skim's first bite went in quickly. The cheap cheese (depressingly savory) coated the inside of his mouth. These surroundings, he thought, would kill it. What a place. It looked like a children's plastic model kit. He imagined the whole building arriving in a box, the same design for everything, down to the salt and pepper pots. His fork bent as it hit the bottom of the pizza. The Muzak dinned in his ear. Nothing seemed real enough. He cursed inwardly. Christ! He should have been explaining what he had to say in some miraculous place.

He decided to leap in. "I do love you in the same way that you love me."

Julia experienced a start of alarm. She was nonplussed; she had no answer for that. It was not what she'd been expecting.

She saw that he was waiting for her assent to allow him to carry on. She said, "Oh."

But for a while Skim merely rushed his food.

Julia calculated how much of her own pizza was left. She wanted to leave as quickly as possible. She was freaked by his wildness. The light in here had done something to his face—made it look more grainy. The pores of his skin were loaded and aiming at her. His hair was corkscrewing wildly. It looked as though a small bomb had gone off a few inches in front of his face.

She could see him working on it still.

"To love someone, right, you have to spend time with them, commit your time to them . . ." He sounded strangled, choked with difficulties and pizza.

212

He waited, watching her, trying to look sensible. "D'you see?" he asked. "I don't live from day to day anymore." Julia didn't reply. She had known for some time that she'd made a mistake with Skim. She felt uncomfortable being cruel. She'd not intended it, or foreseen it. She had held out the knife, yes, but he'd deliberately walked into it. Inside this Pizza Palace cruelty seemed colder, more brittle.

Unable to answer she sat and devalued love, her own love as well—it had never been proven to exist. She'd tried to give it away, but it had never been taken. Others had tried to take it, but then she hadn't been able to give it. The transaction of love, the barter, had never been fully done. Merely squabbled over. Skim was the strangest, bloodiest victim she'd had yet.

She couldn't look at him, he'd become unattractive. His bulk, which previously she'd thought exciting, now made him look clumsy. He was too obviously wounded and running. His grace had gone.

The length of the silence began to panic her. They were stuck with each other at the table, both wrestling with words, but failing. She felt caught in the middle of a silent and motionless storm. She'd have to put her head down and run. Choose any direction and go, somewhere else, anywhere.

She mumbled something about an urgent forgotten appointment and said she'd see him later. Then she fled.

THIRTY-NINE

SANTAY FELT PANIC.

"But where will you *go?*"

"I'm moving back in with those friends."

"But you said . . . but you hated it there."

"I've got nowhere else."

"I bet we'll be all right here for longer than you think. Could be another six months."

"But it might not be."

"It might be. If you hate them . . ."

"You're braver than me. I'll move back there. It won't be for long. I'll find somewhere soon."

"Well, good luck. The best of luck. The best, best, best good luck. Actually I'm looking forward to these last weeks or months or whatever. I mean we can do what we want here. We will have a party every week in a different room, we won't have to clean up afterward and it will still take us three months to work our way round the house. Imagine! It'll be spooky!"

"I can't stay."

"The house will be empty. Talk about being like something out of Dickens. We can play Murder in the Dark."

"Please . . ."

Santay snatched up a handful of trousers in each fist; he tugged at the cloth.

Julia was frightened. "Please . . ."

Santay continued to pull violently at the cloth, his face angry. There was a light squeaking as his wrenching moved the chair.

"Santay . . ."

"Oh Gawwd . . . Bloody, shitty, useless . . ." He yanked his hands off the cloth and pressed the palms against his face, dragging the flesh down.

Julia said, "I won't be blackmailed."

Santay stopped, looking out at her from between his fingers.

"I'm sorry." He felt naked and ashamed.

He found himself logging things: the photos, a letter, books, a packet of computer disks. Julia's telephone number rewritten now on the Weetabix packet.

"It doesn't matter."

As was her habit when there was something to be said which was at all obvious—like this, her goodbye—she didn't say anything. She put her hand in his; it was like a small bird running in there for comfort. After she'd given a brief squeeze she was gone.

Later he heard her struggling in the corridor with her stuff. The slam of the door cut off her conversation with the taxi driver. "Gone," said the slam. "*Gone!*"

Tranquilizers?

It was not a cure, exactly. Going into a drug-induced trance couldn't dispel pity or soothe neediness, but it could go part of the way toward releasing the grip of his mind on the reality of that streaming ticker tape of time that spewed out, marked with his particular code and closely printed with a continuum of information personal to him alone: all bad news.

Or meditation? It couldn't replace sleep, but it made

215

insomnia easier—it was no longer an inch-by-inch search along the barbed-wire boundary of the unconscious.

Meditation. He breathed deeply. He always started at the same point: by imagining that he was stepping into a dark tunnel, then turning to see a light flaring from one end. This corresponded with accounts he'd read in the press of people who had died for a few seconds before returning to life. They had mentioned a tunnel, with a light toward which they had been called. In his meditation he would approach the light, calling once in a while, quietly: "Hello, hello?"

He'd wait for answers, letting them drift through him, hoping for guidance, making his way.

FORTY

⟳☙⟲

GABRIELLA AND MAREK lay sideways on the makeshift bed. The evening had been desultory. The best thing they could think of was to put a stop to it by sleeping.

The gas fire wheezed steadily, squared up to the bed but standing at a lonely distance for safety's sake. Molly's shrouded pile had gone so the room was empty. It had won back the charismatic echoes displaced for so long by her tenancy.

Marek whispered, "Gabriella?"

He could see only the back of her head.

He waited for her to turn to him, but there was nothing, no hand fumbling back to find his. He held on for longer. Perhaps there would be a foot coming, levered back to make conciliatory contact.

"Are you asleep?"

"Mmmm."

"Gabriella?" he murmured, persisting.

"Yes?"

"There's no touching."

He said it as though there were no touchings left, they'd run out of stock. He wanted to order fresh supplies.

Gabriella disentangled the covers from around her neck and turned to frown at him. She swept a hair away from her forehead.

"Are you hot?" he asked.

"No."

"I am. I'm a bit hot."

"Turn it off if you like."

"No, no."

Gabriella wormed her hand under the covers and gently pinched his arm. "I'm sorry."

"Ow."

She found his hand and held it, heaping blame on herself. She'd been wide awake, only pretending to be asleep. She was thinking about her confession. It seemed like a weapon. It belonged to her, but of course Skim had it too, and if she didn't use it, then Skim would . . . She dreaded that more than anything.

A weapon—what sort of weapon? A heavily armored vehicle, breaking cover, trundling into open ground, sitting there and taking the flak, all of it—what's more, it would survive. They might not.

She remembered Mrs. Gorse's warning: "Someone's going to *sew you up!*" Her knees flinched; she closed her eyes.

"So," said Marek. He relaxed his grip on her hand, testing to see if it would stay there.

She had to roll it out one day, this admission, so why not now? She could make excuses: that she didn't realize it was happening; that it had been an affection that had gone wrong because of her inexperience; or that it had happened against her will?

She decided not to attempt any justification. Nothing would do but the bald truth. She liked that expression. Yes, the truth was hairless. Any pleading was desperate, like the thin strands combed over the pate from behind the ear, or a wig bought from a shop and artfully positioned. To make excuses was more disgraceful than lying.

She opened her eyes. Marek was still there, looking at her, holding her hand loosely. The gas fire hissed a warning.

"I love you Marek, I'm more absolutely sure now."

Marek waited.

She continued. "I'm no . . . no unhappy with you, instead with me."

Still Marek hung on.

"I hurt you."

She watched his eyes turn liquid—she could splash her fingers in there; the black water would be warm.

"How?" His whisper was scarcely audible.

"I slipped with Skim."

Marek stared.

"I hurt you, 'aven't I? Have I hurt you? Only once."

Marek was shaken. "Only once?"

"Yes."

A surprise tail quivered between his legs. He had to shrink away from an imagination of the act. He was terrified of asking questions. Quite suddenly her body had a different aura: it was more grown-up than his, different— experienced. He edged forward and claimed a position convolved in her arms—at last he'd got to her skin! He was soothed, frightened . . . He felt himself stiffen with excitement.

Disgust crept over him. He freed himself and sat up.

"What?" asked Gabriella.

Marek got out of bed and walked to and fro in the darkest corner of the room. He didn't want this. It grieved him. He started to look for his clothes.

Gabriella called his name but he didn't answer.

He stood first on one foot, then the other, putting shoes on. He left the room. Darkness, terrible darkness. The cold

219

made the clothes brittle against his skin. Running his fingers on the banister he found his way upstairs and into the bathroom on the first floor, where he cleaned his teeth vigorously.

He returned downstairs, following the walls like a maddened animal. He went into Skim's room, inhaling paraffin fumes. He coughed. His mouth felt clean.

"Hello?" queried Skim, waking, lifting his head.

"It's me, Marek."

Skim turned and sat up.

"Gabriella told me," said Marek.

Skim waited, measuring for mood . . .

"I'm so relieved!" cried Marek. He was gleaming. The truth! He would be armed with knowledge, with experience. He sat on his old bed and trapped his hands to stop them going out to Skim. He wanted to pull him into an embrace.

"I can't tell you," he said, "how happy I am. I am extremely . . . I am happy. Everything has gone—*whoosh*" (his hands were released to flick the air above his head, then returned) ". . . off, all worries gone. I didn't know what was wrong. Now I *know*. I understand everything. I am . . . ah! happy!"

Skim was still waiting.

"Let's go!" said Marek.

"Where?"

"I don't know. Out. Out for a walk!"

Skim gave a considered "OK." He was still testing. He drew back the blankets cautiously. His misused body was there, with only a minimum of clothes on. The thighs looked rude . . . maybe it had been a mistake to reveal them. He wished he could have had a brand-new body. He hurried into the rest of his clothes. "OK, let's go." He lifted the stove up from the ground so the safety mechanism killed the flame with a *clank!* and stumbled out.

220

Marek, still excited, called in a gleeful goodbye to Gabriella. She was startled, and didn't believe in him.

Outside they walked fast to get warm, bobbing among the traffic at the top of the road. Their faces flared in the lights of cars.

The exhilaration kept them close; occasionally their sides nudged together. They fell into a synchronized step: left, right, heading down toward Buckingham Palace. The wall was sheer to the height of three men; the park on the other side was sinister now in the dark. They covered the ground easily together.

They didn't converse much. There were no complications to speak of. Everything was clean—this walk was going to mark a beginning.

At the roundabout outside Buckingham Palace the road widened. The horizon was released with the wall coming to an end; there was parkland now on both sides. A few cars moved at speed down the straight road.

Marek began, "It is great, this news. Like a freedom, like taking off."

"Yes."

The broad satellite road they'd taken out of the roundabout was often used for the pageantry of national events. They celebrated the association, felt the significance of their own occasion grow in scale. Instead of a fanfare they had the rhythmic whisper of their rubber heels striking in unison.

They were halfway down the long, straight road.

"What are you thinking?" asked Skim, wanting to trap the exact truth inside Marek's head at that instant.

"That I have never been so happy," said Marek. "I have everything I wanted, I dreamed about . . . ah! I'm so happy! You must come with us on Thursday." He wanted his friend *with* him.

"How long will Gabriella be in Italy?"

221

"A week or so. We can look after ourselves. Walking, talking, and all."

"I don't know. Term will have started."

"You must. It will be a change of scenery," continued Marek. "I want to go there right now, I want to have wings and fly. I've always wanted to fly—that will be my new hobby, jumping off cliffs and tall buildings, cruising about, then landing again."

They continued, their destination unknown, just wherever, and then back.

When they reached the big square at the end of the road the night traffic was moving more thickly; there was the repressed fury of many engines in competition. The increase in pedestrians, some of them uncontrollably drunk, broke up the unified march of their stride. They found themselves pausing, uncertain.

"Let's go down to the bridge," said Marek.

They walked on.

Skim was trying to think of another word for God. He couldn't use "God"—it had been a swear-word for too long. The whole notion of God and all those stories was, in fact, blasphemous, and the associations were unbreakable. His wasn't a story, so he had to find a new word. The trouble was, there was no other word for it. Bloody God, that's what he'd discovered; it wasn't his fault if everyone else had got it wrong.

Marek was looking up at the tall buildings. Skim couldn't see what was so interesting about the stone façades, but he looked also. They both kept up their odd scrutiny of the blank repetitive patterns of windows.

When they were on the bridge they stopped and looked down, feeling sudden vertigo. The water was sulking blackly round the bottom of the illuminated superstructure. Marek, leaning over, saw in the pattern of the water a face, wrinkled, shadowy, with a swirling expression. With a flourish the sinister mouth spread and curled—was it

222

smiling? No sooner had he spotted it than it disappeared into the flow.

On the other side of the river the streetlights had been more economically spaced. They began to wonder what to say to each other.

Marek dawdled behind. Skim was foxed by this. Every now and again he stopped to wait for Marek to catch up, but he'd only get a brief look from him—Marek's smile would flicker and then fail.

They became disoriented among the warehouses behind the train station. The place had an atmosphere of careless-ness and hard work.

Marek stopped and leaned against a concrete post. He was having difficulties. There was this ridiculous assault by unfamiliar thoughts—he had to defend himself. He waited, watching Skim disappear from sight. Skim then appeared again, retracing his steps. Marek said nothing. He contin-ued to examine the heavens. He couldn't see one star—only a musty industrial blackness.

"Shall we head back?" asked Skim.

"Yes," said Marek, "we'd better go back." He turned to scrutinize Skim, starting with his face. Had they hardened into glass, Skim's eyes, or was he just seeing them as being like marbles because of this change in himself? His inspec-tion dropped to Skim's throat. It was thick like an over-grown leek. Marek felt sick, but he continued to examine Skim. In an ugly way he hungered over every single inch. He could look *through* his clothes. He wanted to destroy the stupidly broad sternum; he wanted to weaken the stout legs that filled the jeans. The shoes had already been punished, he noticed, brazenly overused by the plates-of-meat feet.

What was happening? Marek shook his head to try and clear the unfamiliar hate. He felt as if bewildered by an accident.

On the return journey Marek went to increasing lengths to make sure they walked separately. He hung back. He even thought of going via a different route. The nearer the sight of Skim, the more uncontrollable his obfuscating anger. Was he jealous, was this what it was like? He didn't know what to do with the feeling, how to clamp it down. He searched for some way of doing that. Would it go by itself? He didn't even know what it was, or how much bigger it would grow. "A sickness?" he asked himself. Skim had bewitched him into an utterly foreign mood.

When they were back in the hallway of the house, uncomfortable in the sudden heat of their bodies after the walk, Marek tried to say a small good-night but his voice dried. He couldn't do it.

Skim raised both thumbs.

They parted. Skim went into his room to be greeted by Hawkins, who'd taken his place in the bed.

Marek saw that Gabriella had remained up, waiting for his return. A freshly lit candle burned. The fire exhaled steadily.

Gabriella knew what had happened the moment she saw Marek's fallen face. It was obvious from how opposite his expression was: when he had left, it had been with a lift to each side of his mouth and each eyebrow; now every crease in his skin had dropped.

Gabriella assumed guilt, she shrugged on the old coat again.

Her frown gathered.

FORTY-ONE

Santay closed his eyes. There was a pain there, behind
them—he told it to go. It refused. He rode on the ache, until
it became no more than a pulse, an indication that he was
still alive. His pupils moved behind the lids, relaxing to long
focus.

He began to describe the tunnel in front of him—the
same tunnel as before: oval in shape, dark, but with coruscating sides where the light bloomed at the far end. He
was to walk forward . . . "Hello?"

Ahead of him stood old Mr. Clary, so close to death his
stooping head was already there, brightly lit, skewed upward to enquire into the source of . . .

Life! Life every step of the way, and maybe beyond.
Santay advanced (he could walk, he realized) but then
stopped.

There were some particular people he'd heard about
(Who'd told him? Claude? Yes, Claude): when they decided to die they simply lay down and willed it. They only
had to wait . . .

He wanted to summon them. Would they gather, a quiet, friendly bunch from far-off lands, willing to share their skill and instruct him?

They were all talking at once in a language that sounded like a delirium; he frowned and tried to work out the gist of what they were saying.

Suicide was the only human right. Other rights—food, warmth, justice—however legitimate, were the humblest starting points of privilege, made up of a jostling among wants and haves and expectations. He would resign his right to be involved in life. What a leap. He wasn't far behind old . . .

But perhaps he could overtake old Mr. Clary, put a hand on his horizontal shoulder and step past. Mr. Clary would smile, manage a low wave, follow on at the end of his own good time.

Santay roamed round his corpse to measure the relaxation. He went to his fingers: they were heavy, actually immobile. To his chest to check breathing: shallow, even. Head balancing lightly. All his flesh soaking and heavy with blood. The whole of his interior was thudding and sliding synchronically. To slow it, to stop it altogether would take only a flick of a switch, because that's what the trigger on the pistol was, a switch: life or death, hot or . . .

The trigger worked, the chamber moved round, but the alignment? He remembered Gabriella saying ". . . bang both ways." His hand would get blown off. A sympathetic nerve leapt in his arm. There would be a mess to clean up. It was ugly and unreliable, that weapon.

The excitement had stirred his meditation. Too much. He returned to the beginning; calmed himself. He stepped into the tunnel. It was the same: oval in shape, dark, but with coruscating sides where the light bloomed at the far end. He was to walk forward . . . "Hello?"

The light guided him, he looked directly at it, and at its

226

reflection on the walls. Mr. Clary's foot shifted in the dust as he fidgeted.

His advisers came, as before. They had more instructions. One put a hand on Santay's heart, and counted, murmuring approval as it slowed. The man's head nodded, keeping time. Another watched his breath.

Tranquilizers would offer a kind exit, more of a farewell than a murder of self. There'd be an undignified, greedy session with the two bottles first—pills, drink, more pills, more drink—but then a loosening of tension until every last knot in his nerves slipped, untied itself, fell apart. A final sip of breath. Advantages: one, no violent sights for whoever . . .

But if whoever found him got there early, it was possible he wouldn't be dead. Then, for them, that glorious saving of a life. They'd enjoy that, but the soundness of his mind would have been unpacked by the drugs. It would be impossible to put his brain back together, to get any sense out of himself. That would be the hell of it—to have left to him one miraculously self-contained working eyeball, able to see the caring public as they squinted in and spoke soundlessly.

He calmed himself, breathing, losing the worry by stages, on the outward breaths.

The tunnel was oval in shape, dark, but with coruscating sides where the light . . .

He advanced. Rickety old Mr. Clary was right there, close enough to touch, twisting his head up to welcome him: "Hel. Lo!"

Santay felt one of Mr. Clary's hands on his elbow and he watched the other lift, the antique thumb pointing in the direction of the light. "What. D'you. Think?" The broken-down smile was slow to come, but slower to leave—a lingering, old smile.

Santay felt a folding-together of excitement and prospec-

tive hope, a meltdown in him of all empathy and tender-
ness. God should bless this elderly man.

He stayed deep, in with him.

GABRIELLA CAME AND found him face-down.

"Santay, Santay? It's ten o'clock. Santay?" She called
several times.

"Ahhh . . ."

He lifted his head. A drool of spittle dangled from his
mouth. He was for a moment terrified; he didn't know
where he was or where he'd come from.

"You all right?"

Santay turned his face toward her. It looked stricken with
tiredness.

"Were you in a dream?" she asked.

"I don't know . . . I really don't know." Santay pinned
himself up on his elbows. He rested his forehead back on
the pillow and waited.

Gabriella sat on his bed and watched him wipe his eyes.
It looked too rough, he was digging at them with his
knuckles.

When he next spoke he sounded more in control of
himself. "I feel like I've gone for effing miles. One of those.
I'm not sure if I was asleep, you know, I'm really not
sure . . ."

"Tea, tea," murmured Gabriella, "where is the gaz?"

"Packed it," replied Santay.

"Never mind. I make it in my room and bring it
down."

When she'd gone Santay hauled himself up into a sitting
position. He felt weak. Only the bones were doing the
work, helped by a couple of old dry ligaments—no muscle.
He looked toward the door, listening.

Danger? No.

228

He slid his hand under the mattress. The hardness of the wooden box greeted him. He withdrew his hand.

"Is AMAZING," SAID Gabriella.

"What?"

Marek was cut off from her, somewhere else. She was trying to get him back.

"Santay's done everything. Every bit of packing. Ready to load."

"Oh?"

"Yes. 'Ow dee do it? When?" Gabriella tried to sound cheerful.

Marek didn't answer, so she carried on.

"Yesterday, I s'pose, don't you think? Maybe it was easy. Not much there, really. A few dustbin bags and things."

Marek didn't answer. She left, carrying the tea.

"SANTAY, I DON' wan' to say it too much, but I, you know, I thank you for loaning me the money and . . ."

"Don't mention it again," interrupted Santay. "Two-eighteen. Have a good journey. Write me a card from Italy."

"I 'ave to take your address."

"Oh yes. I'll write it down for you."

She asked, "When are your parents coming?"

"Oh, I don't know, sometime in the evening."

Gabriella stopped writing. "But you say, when I ask you about what time, they are coming before! That can't be, in the evening, how are they going to open the door? There is no one here. You can't get up to open the door . . ."

"Gabriella, I'm not dumb. I've given them keys already. They—have—always—had—keys. I can manage."

Gabriella wore a doubtful expression. "I don' think so.

229

I'm going to change the time of our train, I'm going to catch our later train. We can't live you here alone."

Crisis loomed. She was an irritant, standing above him. The nerves on his neck began to crawl. He felt desperate and tired, so tired. His anger was ruining her. "Look," he said, "I've packed, haven't I? I just want to be able to look after myself. That's all. I don't want people to be hanging about, canceling trains, waiting for me, dealing with me, pushing me about, lifting and carrying me, sitting down with me, the permanent patient."

"I know I know, but you are disable-bodied. You need attention, proper 'tention. You try too hard not to need. I shall stay."

"I'm all right, I'm fucking well all right. I'm a fully grown adult."

"I stay anyway."

"Please, *no*. If something goes wrong I've got a telephone, haven't I?"

He reached under the bed and held the useless instrument aloft. "I can phone if they don't make it."

LATER SANTAY SAW them in the hallway—three figures, all slung with traveling bags. He gave a final wave, and found some ordinary phrases to hurry them along.

Their shuffling, their small voices:

"Have you got tickets?"

"Mmmm?"

"Tickets?"

"Yes. You?"

"Yes."

"Your passport?"

"Yes . . ."

Their organizing became less audible as the front door closed, gently. With the final click of the lock the sound disappeared.

Santay reversed into his room and leaned back in his chair. He dried his sweaty palms along the length of his thighs. The friction heated his hands. Everything sounded abnormally loud. He was the last one left in the house. Not a breath of life except his, moving back and forth, evenly, over his teeth. All systems shut down. He'd been waiting for this—it was a window in time and place. He felt an iota of achievement, through the weariness. He had been determined to organize a quiet suicide, and he'd succeeded.

A nursery rhyme came to his mind—*Where? Here in the chair, right here . . .*

And now he had the time.

Santay wheeled himself to the bed, slid his hand under the mattress, and withdrew the wooden box. He placed it on the bedside table. Carelessly he lifted the lid, like a man who'd used it before. His hands dropped away. It was an ordinary, practical thing that he was doing.

Next he opened the small cupboard below, and pulled out the tranquilizers and brandy.

FORTY-TWO

⟨♥⟩

THEY STROLLED DOWN to Victoria in V-formation—Skim in front, Marek and Gabriella behind.

Marek and Gabriella were hanging back, whispering together. Skim could hear the low, dragging tones of an argument. He turned round once or twice, to see Marek looking at his own feet and to catch guilty looks from Gabriella. They were talking about him. He stayed a tactical distance ahead, for their convenience.

When they reached the station Gabriella had an announcement to make. Turning to face Skim, she wanted to say something else, anything else. So her first two words were heartfelt: "I'm sorry..." but then she glanced at Marek, and became strangely formal, "but I think is best if we don' see each other anymore."

The trains hissed, waiting, powerful tools for traveling.

Skim nodded. Gabriella looked sad; Marek looked hung with shame and disappointment.

"OK," said Skim. "I did wonder. Never mind." He surveyed the scene. "It's just as well," he continued awkwardly. "Term's started and I've hardly done a day's work."

"What will you do?"

"Go back to the house for a bit . . . I don't know. I'll go. I'll go. You've got to go—look at the time. Off . . . yes, go! Goodbye. Good luck." He shooed them angrily, waving his hands until they turned and left him.

He stood there with his new bag.

They hurried; the practicalities of doors and cases relaxed the situation for a while but the row they'd been having for two days came back to haunt them once they were on their way. Having found seats they sat in silence.

The train rattled. A late-afternoon sun polished selected surfaces, sliding along one thing before moving to another.

"Wearily wearily wearily . . ." thought Marek. He was relieved—Skim was gone. The relief allowed him to feel tired.

Again the door behind his shoulder opened; the same abrupt blast of air and noise just as abruptly stopped. Marek glanced up and saw—

Skim.

"I suddenly thought," murmured Skim in a low voice, "that I had to come along. We've got to spend some time together, we have, you and I."

Marek stared. The woman next to him stopped chewing. She looked at them suspiciously.

"Mmm?"

"I think we've got to spend more time with each other, give ourselves more time."

Marek was polite again: "All right." He nodded. He even concocted a little laugh.

There was no seat available nearby so Skim passed down the corridor. Marek turned to Gabriella and saw her mouth shaped in a small O.

Skim felt careless. He didn't mind about this conflict with his friend. It seemed quite trivial, very short-term. He could wait. He had all the time in the world. Eternity! He could happily open up his wrists and spray this woman in front of him who was listening so politely. It would be a game. Nothing mattered . . .

"Yes . . ." The strange voice was replying to him, feigning interest.

Hate moved like an unwelcome worm in Marek's food. Hate! He was still incredulous that such a well-muscled squirming thing had introduced itself into his bowels. The hammering of the train annoyed him—a stupid rhythm. He would cherish an escape. He longed for complete silence.

Gabriella looked across at Marek's doleful expression opposite her. He was looking out of the window, his eyes flicking with crazy speed as he snatched glimpses of things going past the window.

The three of them (trying for comfort) milled about in the crowded train, looking for something to divert them. Marek went on a trip to the food bar. Skim followed. Marek returned empty-handed, he couldn't stick it in the queue; Skim came back with cake.

When they arrived in Rochester it was dark. They hired a taxi to reach the borrowed flat, which was above a shop on High Street selling tools and DIY materials. It was owned by one of Marek's tutors, who'd inherited it, a granny flat without a granny.

They divided and went to their rooms. Skim was the odd man out—alone. He wasn't too worried. He thought it would come right eventually. He was conscientiously adding up hours and waiting to be included. It was like being in the wilderness. Jesus had been in the wilderness for forty days and forty nights. Ah—but he'd never been in the doghouse. Skim was in the doghouse. He gave himself one point up on Jesus' score.

He no longer hated all these religions. They hadn't lost their stupidity, no, but they had a certain sort of misguided charm. It was magical: people had so much felt God should exist that they had been forced to invent—and such fantastic stories. It made him feel warm. It didn't matter that perhaps no one would ever know the truth but him. *He* knew, that's what counted.

MAREK LAY ON the bed and watched Gabriella as she tilted her head back to rest against the blindingly clean white wall. He judged his private feeling: unfair. Why did he not hate Gabriella as well? Why did he love her more than ever, when she had betrayed him more finely, more perfectly, than Skim ever could? He lay with his hands behind his head, and looked down to his toes. His body had been stolen, that animal had sneaked in . . . He was sure his feet looked hairier. The familiar tears started rising. He even despised his own tears now whereas before he had thought they were evidence of talent. He had never known such an inward, personal unhappiness. It gripped so persistently. Was this it, was he going to have to live with this? He gripped the back of his head as it was there lying in his hands. He wanted to crack it like it was an egg, then he could go in with a spoon and change his brain, swap it for someone else's, or leave it out altogether. Put it in a jar.

FORTY-THREE

SANTAY CURSED, OVER and over again. He pressed the bullets into the chamber, his hands fumbling; he expected them to explode and take his fingers off. With the gun in his lap he wheeled himself to the far side of the room. He turned to face the door.

The hammering stopped. He heard a voice complaining, "Willya stoppit?"

"Stop what?"

"Stoppit now."

There was silence, then the sound of more effort in the hallway. Santay continued to swear noiselessly, holding the gun tightly in his hands. Who were these men? What were they doing?

"I said stoppit."

"What?"

"Stop pestering me."

"You—you're always sayin that, 'Willya stoppit.' I could call you Willya Stoppit."

"I'm only always sayin' it because you're on to teasin' me all the time with your friggin' pinchin' my belly. Stoppit!"

236

"Come on Willya Stoppit, you should be done with that now. Come on."

"What do you know? We've got downstairs as well. Get out to the van and make yourself useful."

Footsteps. Santay secured an amateur grip on the pistol. The voices were outside the house—but then there were more footsteps coming back in. Santay concentrated on the door—on the door handle. One of the men was coming down the three stairs toward his room. A grimace was fixed on Santay's face. He looked at the black eye of the barrel. It looked cold, it looked dead, that eye. He drew it up. A touch . . .

FORTY-FOUR

For their first evening meal they stayed at home and cooked omelettes. Marek started to chop the onions. The knife was sharp, very sharp. The knife might slip.

As the fumes began to bite he cursed under his breath, "I don't believe it." It was tactless of Gabriella to give this job to him and make his eyes smart again. He looked down at the blurred onions. They were themselves like large eyes moving loopily round the room.

Skim got the first omelette and tucked himself under the table close to Marek. Marek felt swamped by anger. The sheer rowdy size of Skim's body. Marek hated the noise he could hear: the business of Skim's eating. The proximity of the man was an electric charge fluttering in a jealous corner of his brain. When his own omelette came he picked at it for a while before wandering over to the sink. He was washing up and eating at the same time.

Gabriella made a suggestion: they should walk to the nearby pub and see what was there. No one disagreed.

They strolled up the road in the dark. There—Marek pulled ahead slightly. Gabriella had the sensation that a huge crowd of people was watching her. She didn't want to be seen hurrying after him, but at the same time she didn't want to be seen hanging back with Skim. She took up a middle position. Her one call to Marek made him stop and turn round, but only to wave momentarily before continuing. Gabriella held both her arms up in the air: her reply. It was a curious display.

They sat in the pub, drinking a little. A man started up with his guitar. He said a few words, introducing the song. Everyone applauded in anticipation, and even more enthusiastically after he'd finished. He was waved over to accept a pint.

A while later Skim went and spoke to him; he smiled as they talked. He glanced back to Marek, indicating with his thumb. The musician followed Skim back and handed the guitar to Marek with a flourish.

Marek took the instrument, smiling politely. He played a few chords and altered the tuning, then again he strummed the same few chords. The pub went quiet.

"No, no . . . I can't," he said. He handed it back to the stranger.

Marek and Gabriella sat together in silence, their glasses empty.

Marek made the effort to look at Skim (he had thought of a possible way out). He said, "Maybe it's more time apart we need, rather than time together."

Skim was pursing his lips round the rim of his glass, lowering the pint, and nodding as he swallowed the liquid.

"Time apart? Interesting idea. Could be, could be."

They fell back to silence.

When they were on their way home Marek broke into a trot and disappeared from sight, gathering speed. Gabriella accelerated into a fast walk. Skim dropped a little behind.

Gabriella found Marek lying spread-eagled on the carpet in their bedroom, as though he'd fallen from a great height. He was naked.

"Marek? Marek?"

He didn't answer her. He lay there, determinedly motionless.

She put a hand on his shoulder, but then withdrew it—she didn't try to turn him. She stayed sitting next to him for some time, listening to Skim's bathroom noises.

SKIM WENT TO bed, and, being a little drunk, he fell asleep practicing encounters with famous people. He put himself up for a visit to the Pope. He'd been invited! What would he have to do? Kiss the ground? No, kiss the ring...

The ring came up to his face and he moved to it unsalaciously. He saw that a place had been laid for him at the table. The Pope waved him to his seat. A serving of Italian biscuits waited in the middle.

"You see," said the Pope, pointing an enormous index finger at the biscuits and smiling kindly, "I have heard about you."

The Pope poured the tea with fastidious ceremony. For a while they would converse intelligently about current issues, drinking tea and eating the sophisticated crumbles. The Pope was listening, nodding, impressed with Skim's raw but certain understanding of life.

Then there was a pause, and the Pope would brush crumbs from his frock. Skim recognized that a serious moment had arrived.

"I've invited you here for a particular reason," said the Pope, "and I dare say you already know what that reason is."

"I think so, Your Honor." Skim gloried in the stateliness of the man.

"I want you to explain to me," continued the Pope gravely, "your idea about God and Time being ... being the same *thing*." A brief worry, or doubt, came to the Pope's face.

Skim flushed with pride. One leg bounced nervously

as he began, but when he saw that the Pope was locked onto his every word he became confident; eloquence was lent to him from some mysterious source. The Pope grew astonished at the bare-faced facts, the obviousness, the truthfulness, spilling from the lips of this ordinary, untutored working man.

Skim came to the end of his remarkable thesis. A silence was held by both of them. A monk appeared to clear away the tea and winked at Skim.

The Pope, meanwhile, was racing through a lifetime's learning in theology, matching certain lines of opinion across the ages. He abandoned his chair and walked thoughtfully for a few paces, his knuckles pressed against his teeth.

A moment of indecision.

Urgently, the Pope reached behind his neck. The folds of his goiter wobbled over the collar—then it was off, a ring of white on the polished wood floor.

No. The Pope didn't wear a dog collar. What would it be, the permanent high fashion of his particular ceremony? Oh yes.

"Unzip me!"

Skim did what he was told.

The Pope stepped neatly out of his frock and kicked it aside. His shoe flew off, clattering some way off.

A bell began ringing. Voices shouted. They would have to escape.

It was easy enough. They slipped past the pursuing monks and found a back door. Outside in the sunshine they strode about, talking man to man. They went to a café. People stared at the Pope—they didn't recognize him, but he looked odd, wearing ankle socks and a papal underwear set.

MAREK COULDN'T SETTLE to sleep. It was a strange bed, a new room. He was in and out of nightmares, waking up to

241

find himself grilled with anxiety. Gabriella was the only other person in the room? He interpreted the shadows, finding sensational answers for them all. He got up and walked about, trying to teach himself that he was all right.

In the kitchen, with the cold floor numbing his feet, he stood on curled toes and tipped back a glass of water in great slugs. He felt it chill his innards on the way down. That was better. He stood by the window. Air stroked the hairs on his legs. Nerves stirred in various lairs on his body—in the small of his back, across his shoulders, on his chest. He shivered. A tickle persisted in his nose.

He went and stood outside Skim's room, listening.

EARLY THE NEXT morning, before Skim was up, Marek went with Gabriella to the station. She was going to continue her journey to Italy, then she'd return and meet him in Rochester.

"I can't go back," said Marek.

Gabriella waited, her case dragging down one shoulder.

"I'm not going to go back," he repeated, "it's impossible. I'm not going back to that flat."

"Where will you go?"

"I don't know. To Italy?"

She looked at him, perplexed, shaking her head. "Why not London?"

"All right, London. I'll be in London."

"Where?"

"Chapel Street."

"You can no go there now, really."

"I'll go there. Please, where else?"

"You can stay at Claude and Molly."

"Maybe. But maybe not."

"I muss get on my train. What shall we do?"

"I'll leave where I am, my address, with Mrs. Gorse. When you get back, ring Mrs. Gorse . . ."

Gabriella was climbing aboard. A guard closed the door on her. She put her head through the window. "OK, Mrs. Gorse . . ."

"We'll go through Mrs. Gorse . . ."

"Yes."

He watched until the train weaned him of her, passing out of sight.

Back at the flat he took his few things and packed them again. Walking in socks so as not to wake Skim, he went to the kitchen to write a note. It was a thoroughly everyday set of instructions to do with the keys! This amazed him.

Alone, squeezed among commuters, he caught an early train back to London.

The city was heartlessly crowded. He wandered aimlessly around his favored landmarks and dialed people from cold and sticky phoneboxes, but no one answered him.

Later, his feet aching from the long hours of aimless walking, he approached the environs of Chapel Street with misgiving. He stopped, and swapped his bag to the other hand. It wasn't far.

Chapel Street . . .

He realized he couldn't bear to go there either, not to that house. He turned back, taking random streets toward the poorer areas of Victoria. He was scouting for a bed-and-breakfast.

Dusk closed down the square of light coming from his rented window. He knew that he would be unable to eat or read in the strange room, or do anything but try and dredge his mind to bring to the surface some opinion of what had happened to him. His personality, he thought, had been soiled. He despaired of finding a link between what he found himself to be now, and what he had been when, for instance, he had made the candle holders. The potential of failure, any real emotional failure, had, back then, been an invisible door that he'd been blindly on his way toward

243

opening. On the other side of the door this science fiction landscape of despair had been awaiting him. Here he stood, up to his neck!

He switched the lights on. With a leaden sense of timing one of the light filaments sputtered and died in the bottom of its glass bulb.

He began to doodle on a piece of paper, working at the shading of what turned out to be a skull with its mouth open. He refined its expression and found himself making guesses: it had died, yes. After a long-suffered illness. After a week's torture and burning. The permanent fixedness of the expression, its exact exaggeration of Marek's own feelings, gave him some maudlin satisfaction as he climbed into the strange bed. His limbs only willingly obeyed gravity.

As he lay there the face began to frighten him. It peeled itself off the page and girned at him, aping death. It looked like Death. Perhaps it *was* Death.

He sank a notch further toward sleep. Then he woke again, sweating. He shouldn't have thought about death. Now he had to put up with the discomfort of an adrenaline-laden system . . .

He was so tired. He was bogged down in fatigue, halted by carrying so much bewilderment, exhausted from chasing hope.

Later, when he was leaning gently against the furthermost outposts of sleep, just at the point of trusting himself enough, his heart stopped.

It was a falling, the depths yawned, he knew there was no limit, nothing to bring him up. In the same moment it came to him that the face had done this.

It was an emergency. He opened his mouth, itself a hole that he was in danger of falling into, and from within came an awful tone of sound. The noise came involuntarily from his vocal cords, as though they were vibrating by themselves without air passing over them. His rise toward the surface was a life-and-death struggle to save himself from the hollowness of that sonorescence. He arrived, finding himself jerking into a sitting position, breathing hard. He couldn't see himself in the blackness. Did he exist? Yes . . . Yes was the answer. A mournful wave of discontent dragged at him, a virulent undertow. He was alive.

Failing to calm down, he got up and went out for a walk. He played a word-association game: bridge—river; pedestrian—walking; streetlight—spy . . . He thought he might be about to faint, there was such a dizziness in his thoughts. The bridges confused him—there were so many. He turned away from the river and kept walking.

He cursed. How could he get out of this loss?

Hours later he had come round in a circle to another bridge (bridge—river; river—face; face—); he began to cross.

He paused halfway over the bridge and leaned against the rounded iron balustrade, looking over the side. Face— Face what? He was stuck.

Then he heard a voice.

"Go on mate, jump!"

He turned to his left and saw two young men lounging against the parapet a little farther up the slope of the bridge. They were the only people. They waved, harmlessly enjoying the night outside.

Marek leaned forward.

"Go on!"

Marek heard their voices, and examined what they were saying as though from an objective, incurious distance. He was pivoting on his stomach. The black paint on the heavy ironwork was slippery.

"Wo wo wo!" The men hooted encouragement.

Marek tipped himself further forward. A gallon of blood was gathering in his head. His upside-down eyes felt like they were about to burst; they would pop from their sockets and drop into the river below. His lips, overfull, stung. He could feel his hair waving at the water.

"Yah yay!" cried the young men.

Marek swung himself back onto his feet. The world careered; a car fled past. "Ahhh . . ." crooned the two youths, the cadence of the car and their cry dwindling together to nothing.

"*Bonky,*" Marek whispered, his midriff aching, "fucking *Bonky.*"

He started walking, slowly. If he followed the river he'd come to Victoria Station. He fished the timetable from his pocket.

To the youths watching from the bridge he became no more than a shape moving in and out of the streetlights.

SKIM HAD FOUND the note on the kitchen table. Yes, he left the keys with the DIY shop manager, but then he departed from the written instructions. He followed Marek's route.

So he sat on the train and ate sandwiches. To him the globe had become comfortingly small; he was happy that his particular trial had taken on real geographical scope. There was no one else in his compartment so he spread himself over the seats. He felt like a single soldier, in an army of one. His mission was ringing in his head, calling for him. He would be capable of undergoing any form of torture, he wanted to wear a thousand scars; some of them would be new. He listened to the noise of the train's hooves beneath him, reveling in the trundling changes of rhythm. He imagined wings growing out from the side of the train. It would lift off and climb into the air at an angle of forty-five degrees; the iron horse would fly.

When he arrived at Chapel Street he was greeted by Hawkins, who miaowed angrily and trotted toward him, looking tough in the new studded collar that Skim had bought. It wasn't like Hawkins to be out here. He should still have been eating all the great piles of food Skim had left for him—enough to last for the week.

Skim began to see a possible reason. He cranked himself up the three front steps. There was a contractor's sign nailed to the door: JOHN LELLIOTT AND SONS. He inserted his key but it didn't turn—the locks had been changed. He cursed. His tools, stolen?

He wound down the outside steps to try the basement. The door he'd kicked down had been replaced (sure enough, the new one didn't have a cat flap).

Skim made a nest for Hawkins in his coat and climbed the steps back onto Chapel Street. He paused, considering which way to turn.

He would have to find a place for himself.

INSIDE THE HOUSE, it was silent. There was no footstep or voice, no noise of the water queueing to make its way round the antique network of lead and copper pipes. There was rubbish strewn about, like a wind had blown through. The walls stared openly. Silence. The house was saying nothing. It still had secrets, but there were no questions.

Parked heavily in Santay's doorway was a rat. Its eye stared dully.

Santay's wheelchair was there, ready for use and indented by years of carrying his shape—but it was incongruously empty.

His body was lying face-down on the bed, and looked gutted, the physical collapse was so utterly definite. There was no anger to it, rather a concentrated acceptance. It was partly an effect of how the legs were positioned: bent at the knee, but separated, as though caught in a running jump. The hands were curled together, partially obscuring the face (the hair still growing).

On the table by the bed stood a radio, a cup, a quart of

247

brandy, a dark brown bottle of pills with a childproof cap, and the wooden box, open, with the pistol lying in its fitted interior. The matrix of bullets (positioned just under the barrel) was complete.

The pills, too, were untouched; the fat plug of cotton wool wormed down onto the tablets.

Already the skin was drawn closer to the shape of the skull. The mouth tightening.

Santay had simply aimed here, toward death, knowing it was the immaterial equivalent of gravity: the most persistent magnetic force drawing on life. And it led to the same thing, the same place. A black hole—Time's lair.

There they were, escaped, or trapped, or waiting: all dead souls. They stood mournfully. Fathers, mothers, grandparents, all of them children once. What was it they were holding? Messages? Squares of paper held out . . . Their lips moved as they tried for their stories.

They were showing photographs. This gave Santay an inward smile. Other people's photos!